D0699696

DANGEROUS ARRIVALS

DANGEROUS ARRIVALS

Ted Allbeury

severn House

This title first published in Great Britain 2007 by
SEVERN HOUSE PUBLISHERS LTD of
9–15 High Street, Sutton, Surrey SM1 1DF.
Originally published 1975 in Great Britain only
under the title *Where All the Girls are Sweeter*
and under the pseudonym of *Richard Butler*.
This title first published in the USA 2007 by
SEVERN HOUSE PUBLISHERS INC of
595 Madison Avenue, New York, N.Y. 10022.

British Library Cataloguing in Publication Data

Allbeury, Ted
  Dangerous arrivals
  1. Italy - Fiction 2. Suspense fiction
  I. Title
  823.9'14[F]

ISBN-13: 978-0-7278-6518-2   (cased)

Except where actual historical events and characters are being
described for the storyline of this novel, all situations in this
publication are fictitious and any resemblance to living persons
is purely coincidental.

All Severn House titles are printed on acid-free paper.

Typeset by Palimpsest Book Production Ltd.,
Grangemouth, Stirlingshire, Scotland.
Printed and bound in Great Britain by
MPG Books Ltd., Bodmin, Cornwall.

This book is dedicated to my grandparents, Albert Edward and Mary Bailey. They are long since dead, but it's to mark their many years of gentleness and kindness to me when I was a boy.

Although nothing was ever expected, I know in retrospect that I gave far too little back.

One

The girl perched on the bar stool had performed a small miracle. At six o'clock on any evening the Bar di Corso was loud with the sagas of deals done, bargains struck, and the latest jokes about the Vatican. But now, apart from a shifting of uneasy backsides on rickety chairs and a deal of heavy breathing, the place was silent. The Bar di Corso was not a place frequented by women. It wasn't intended for women. Not that it wasn't perfectly respectable, but no woman had ever drunk there in twenty years. So any girl would have generated enough astonishment to halve the noise level, but this one had brought the place to a silent standstill. She had asked for a whisky and when an astonished padrone had admitted this basic lack she'd settled for a brandy. Every eye had been on her glass as she took the first slug. From then on they'd stayed on her. She was in her early twenties with long blonde hair and a face that was so beautiful that nothing more was needed. But nature so often overdoes things and her thin cotton shirt did nothing to conceal the full breasts with their visibly genuine tips. And the tight blue faded jeans clung to the long, curving thighs till her smooth, shapely calves were revealed where the jeans had been cut just below her knees. As far as the girl was concerned, she could have been unaware of the devastation she had caused, except that having taken the rest of her drink in one easy throw she bent down for a canvas duffle bag and walked slowly to the door and turned towards the line of hotels. But if you're unaware you don't need to give the boys that extra swish of an already gorgeous backside.

Then, as if the good Lord had pressed a switch, there was the thunder of two dozen Italian men registering their disbelief and appreciation. The consensus had it that she was *un' Americana*. And then they got down to the wondrous details. Scientific studies show that four witnesses to an event cannot give an accurate description of what went on. But the Bar di Corso buried that theory deep, and for ever. Nobody'd missed a thing and they could describe it all in prose or poetry, with metric measurements.

I waited another half-hour for Mario and then wandered along to the fish market, bought a couple of plaice and headed for the boat.

She was a thirty-foot Fjord, built in Norway, with two hefty Volvo diesels, and I'd sold her to a man in the rag-trade. Part of the deal was that I delivered her from Chichester to Santa Margherita. I'd brought a bottle for the harbour master and that got me an alongside berth and saved me the trouble of using the dinghy. It was going to take me a week to spruce her up. The pulpit and stanchions were encrusted with salt and the GRP hull and super-structure were grey instead of white. The lifting mechanism on the port engine had jammed and the VHF radio needed a new crystal. My faded red ensign would go back with me. The new owner belonged to one of the fancy yacht clubs and used a blue ensign. And kept it up all night. He was bringing it with him when he handed over his present gin-palace that wasn't seaworthy beyond Canvey Island.

If it wasn't for the hotels and the mayor, you wouldn't even be able to call Santa Margherita a town. They used to bring in the holidaymakers in Short Sunderlands that landed right in the bay. But now you have to use the train or the coast bus from Genova, so it's become more exclusive, and they arrive with Mercs, Rolls-Royces or Jags. This was the sixth boat I'd brought to Santa Margherita and, with a month on leave here at the end of the war, I felt like an old China hand.

Nearly an hour later somebody called my name and I came up out of the saloon. It was Mario and he looked like something out of *The Great Gatsby*. A dark jacket with gilt buttons, white slacks and a pair of white and tan co-respondent's shoes. A tribute to the British way of life. He settled himself down in one of the chairs on the after-deck, beaming his big Italian smile. I'd been liaison officer to his group of partisans near La Spezia in the days when a Special Operations Executive supplied the arms and know-how, and called the tune.

When I'd poured him a drink, he patted the teak bulk-head.

'This all yours, Max?'

'This is the one I sold to Dixon. The guy I put in touch with you.'

Mario was ship's husband to almost everything that sailed into Santa Margherita and Portofino. He'd got a piece of most of the marine action on that bit of coast. But he claimed it with charm and amiability, and even at fifty-five he looked younger than most men of thirty. His thick black curly hair was wiry and sprinkled with grey, and he had an old-fashioned Fairbanks-type moustache. And the grin with the big white horse's teeth still did things for the girls.

'There's a German guy staying at the Lido. He wants a Chris Craft or a Grand Banks. Maybe you help him?'

'What size does he want?'

'Thirty foot or thirty-five. Petrol or diesel he not mind.'

'OK, I can fix him up.'

He smiled and started to lift his glass and then something on the quay caught his eye. He slowly put the glass back on the chart-table. The saloon door blocked my view so I stayed put. Even when he said, *'Mamma mia! Che bella ragazza, che carena. Guardi la figura e le gambe . . .'*

When he was halfway down the bill of fare I pushed the louvred door aside with my foot. It was the young blonde from the café. When she saw me, she bent down and the long blonde hair touched her knees.

'Are you the Englishman?'

'What Englishman?'

'Can you give me a bunk for the night? I'll pay.'

One rule I have, I don't make a quick buck with a client's boat. A hundred dollars for a day's unmentioned charter can lose you a whole line of boat sales. But the trim young blonde was a lovely, and maybe she could cook more than fish fingers.

'Can you cook?'

The long blonde hair shook in slow motion like a TV shampoo ad.

'No, mister. No can do.'

'Why not fix a motel room, sweetie? The old lady at the beach kiosk will do you a room cheap.'

She squinted at me with one grey eye as the low sun shone on her face. Then she sighed and stood up slowly and reached for the duffle bag. She looked very young, and her wrists were vulnerable and slender like the stalks of daffodils. She was turning away when I called out.

'Come down and have a drink.'

She slipped off her sandals and stepped on to the slotted plank that led from the quayside to the boat. There was almost no movement because I'd warped her tight and the girl hopped down on to the seat cushion and then down to the teak grating of the after-deck. She reached over to the quay for the duffle bag and Mario did his stuff and swung it down for her. Then with a broad grin he stepped down on to the plank and stood on the quay and waved.

'*Ciao*, Max, *a domani – a la dieci.*'

The girl sat in the flowered chair with one foot on the canvas bag and she leaned down to clean the dirt and sand from her bare feet. I went down in the saloon and poured her a whisky. When she'd had the first sip, I started.

'What's your name, honey?'

She answered without looking up.

'Tammy.'

'Tammy what?'

'Just Tammy.'

And then she did look up.

'Which d'you want, a screw or the story of my life?'

I looked at the pretty face. Her big grey eyes were the colour of sliced gooseberries. There were flecks in them but I couldn't make out the colour of these. Her nose was neat with smooth nostrils, and her mouth was wide with full soft lips. She didn't blink under the stare or turn her face away.

'Which would *you* prefer, Tammy, baked beans or fried eggs?'

And when she smiled I felt foolishly pleased.

'Beans on toast?'

'On toast it is. Grab your bag and come on down.'

I fished down in the bilge for a tin. There was just one left with a label and that was chilli con carne. I opened three before I hit the jackpot. I'm good at beans. I've had plenty of practise. For me it's 'Give us this day our daily beans'. There was still a slab of Sainsbury's Normandy butter and I topped off with a good slice. She ate like she was still at school, while I made two cups of instant coffee.

The foam seats each side of the saloon table were comfortable and as I settled on the other side she leaned back and stretched out those long legs. She looked around the saloon without much interest. I offered her a cigarette but she shook her head, and her hair did it all over again.

'What made you come to this boat?'

She looked at me for quite a time before she spoke.

'I was scared.'

'What of?'

'I don't really know. I'd made some arrangements and something went wrong. Can I stay here for a couple of days?'

She wasn't going to answer anything, but it didn't really matter.

'Sure.'

I played her at Scrabble for two hours and she played dirty. Put down 'ax' as a word, and when I challenged her, there it was in my *Chambers' Twentieth Century.* A girl who would do that needs watching. When the pieces were all crammed up in one corner we called it a day. As I was putting it all away she said, 'A lot of people here seem to know you. You sell boats, don't you?'

'Yep. Sell 'em and buy 'em. To me I always seem to be buying but I guess to the rest of the world it seems like I'm only selling. They're the next best thing to . . .' and I stopped. But I couldn't think of a realistic alternative. She was smiling so I got back on top again and said, 'You like to go for a stroll before you turn in?'

And suddenly it was like having a daughter. The slugger down of brandy was all excitement at going for a walk. I held her hand as we negotiated the plank to the quay because there was a slight swell now and it seemed natural to keep on holding it as we walked towards the lights. When we got to the street there were lights in the line of trees and I whistled up Giovanni and his *carrozza.* He trotted us down to Portofino. We had *gelati* and black coffee and were back at the boat about eleven.

As we went down the companionway to the saloon

she had her hands on my shoulder. The boat was rocking slightly as we stood at the bottom of the steps and when I turned round and looked at her face the big goosegog eyes knew exactly what I was thinking and they weren't saying no. I thought hard of graveyards and terrible wounds and kissed her cheek. Then back in command.

'OK, Tammy. The for'ard bunk is yours. I'm going to be outside in the nice fresh air.' And the silly bitch said, 'OK, Captain, whatever you say.'

I closed the two doors and settled down in a sleeping bag on the after-deck. For about twenty minutes I kept one ear in the fresh air in case she came wandering out to snuggle down with me like they do in books. But it was just me and the mosquitos. Ten minutes trying not to think about what the machinery would look like without the shirt and jeans. And then half an hour thinking about it with no inhibitions and in glorious Technicolour. By then she was snoring and not like a baby either. More like a drunken scrum half.

Two

The wind must have backed in the night because at three in the morning the boat was snatching at the mooring. It took fifteen minutes to adjust the mooring lines and put on a couple of springs. There were lights on some other boats where the hired hands were doing their stuff.

When I'd finished I went up on to the quay to check the fenders. It was very dark and I leaned over carefully to lengthen the fender ropes till they were holding off the rubbing strake from the wall. I stood up and stepped back to check the ropes on the bollard. A hard-edged voice said, 'Don't move, Mister, just freeze,' and a gun jerked at the bottom of my back. He must have been standing in the shadow of the wall, waiting for me. I leaned back very slightly and my backbone touched the muzzle immediately. Shoving a gun against somebody's back is not a very bright thing to do unless you're dealing with amateurs. Guns aimed at backs should be more than an arm's length away. 'Just walk down there, Mac, and go very slow.' He used the gun to punctuate and I took three paces, rolled round his

9

hand, locked his arm and gave him what the judo boys call a 'reap' and his arm cracked loudly as he went down on his back. With his good arm he grabbed my legs and I went with him, one knee in his groin and the other in his belly. As I went for his throat I missed and he rolled. With a broken arm that was a mistake, and I shoved both my hands under his jaw and linked my fingers as I pulled his head back. When the intelligence group at Beaulieu taught you how to kill men without making a noise they did just that. And I pulled against the fulcrum of my knee and his body shuddered as the spinal cord was trapped and then severed by the bones. They didn't tell you how to do anything short of killing. Two of the fingers on my left hand were dislocated and hanging in the wrong direction and my right eye was closed. There was warm blood coming from somewhere on my head. And my heart was beating so fast that I couldn't get off his back. Then Tammy was there, white-faced and shaking.

'My God, Max, what's happened?' And I stood up unsteadily and she held me upright. There was a thumping like big diesels in my head but the fog was clearing. When I could speak, I waved her to the ladder.

'Tammy, go down in the saloon. Put the key on your side and lock the doors. Don't answer or let anyone in except me. I'll knock the V sign for you – you know, da-da-da-daa, like in the war.'

'What are you going to do, Max? God, look at your fingers – and your face.'

'I'm going for the police but I want a look at my friend first. Now, do as I tell you – quickly.'

10

I rolled the man over on to his back. He was about six feet, well-built, balding, with thin black hair. His eyes were open but the damage to his nervous system had turned his pupils up into his head. His hands were rough and calloused. He was about forty to forty-five. I'd seen faces like his all round the world. They were the muscle boys for top crooks. But they relied on surprise and guns and their combination of brute force and brute brains left them at a disadvantage with anyone who was trained. They were beaters-up, not fighters. This boy had too many chins and too much paunch.

There were the usual odds and ends in his pocket but the inside jacket pocket had a letter and a thick wallet held together by a wide elastic garter. I dragged him into the shadow of the stone wall and went slowly, one-handed, down the ladder to the boat. I did the old 'V' sign and Tammy opened up. I had a double whisky and it took me ten sweating minutes to get my fingers back into their sockets. They went in easily enough but the internal swelling made them loose. I taped all the fingers of that hand into a solid pad.

In the wallet was £180 in sterling notes, a couple of pornographic photographs, a driving licence for Montague C. Dodds, a cutting from the racing page of the *Daily Mirror* and the return half of a train ticket from Milan.

The envelope was thin brown manilla and typed on the front was 'Personal to P.S. Dixon'. I put the electric kettle on and slid a table knife under the flap as it eased open in the steam. I laid the flap back and let it dry before I took out the letter, which was typed on good white paper. It said:

We saw it coming, Dixon. You're not that good.
Give the details to Monty. Don't play games.
D.T.

I kept the letter and cutting from the *Daily Mirror* and stuffed the odds and ends and the wallet back in his jacket. Then I reported to the *questura* and they weren't as thrilled as I'd expected. They took photographs and measurements and popped things into plastic bags. They took a statement from me and from Tammy and then they went. No warnings about not leaving the country or threats of arrest. It seemed that even in Santa Margherita they'd done it before. I didn't mention the letter to the police.

It was two in the morning when I got back to Tammy. We chatted round the evening minus Monty and then she suddenly said, 'Why'd you have to kill him, Max?'

'I don't like guys who pull guns on me, honey.'

'But you could have taken the gun off him.'

'Look, my love, if people put a gun in my back then what happens afterwards is their worry.'

'But you could have knocked him out or something.'

'I don't know how to knock men out who put guns in my back. But I do know how to kill 'em.'

'Why do you think he was here?'

I shook my head to add conviction to the lie.

'I've no idea, honey. Maybe he was just thieving. Where there's boats you often get this. They pick up radios and compasses. I've known them go down a line of boats and strip them, outboard engines and all.'

She didn't look entirely convinced but I left it at

that. One thing was for sure. Whatever Dixon might think, I was going to pay a little visit to the bastards who had sent Montague Dodds down to Santa Margherita with a gun. There must be a bit of Israeli blood somewhere in my bloodstream. My motto is an eye for an eye. If you don't hit them back, they might try it again.

There wasn't much moon but up on the hill at the back of the town you could see the white fronts of some of the big villas, pale and ghostly in the quiet darkness. The only noise was the quick slapping of the waves against the boat's smooth hull.

I didn't wake until after seven and there was no noise from the saloon. I'd got some gear at Mario's place and I changed while he brewed up some tea. He'd been hooked ever since I brought him some Tetley's teabags last year.

'Who's the German who wants a boat, Mario?'

'Herr Paulos. Makes office equipment in Frankfurt. Taken a villa by the old bridge.'

'What's he got to trade-in?'

'Nothing – it's a clean deal.'

'Does he want a marine mortgage?'

'No. He pay cash in dollars or Deutsch mark.'

'Is that Meakes Sea Lion at Camogli still for sale?'

'Yeah, but the widow's too greedy, she wants forty thousand dollars. Too much money, Max. You make no profit on that.'

The widow and the Sea Lion took nearly two hours. Mario was wrong. It was in good nick but a year's weather had made it scruffy. I took an option on it for twenty-four hours at thirty-five thousand dollars and walked to the German's villa. It was getting hot. I looked at my sweaty wrist. It was nearly 11.30.

Herr Paulos was in his fifties. Not what I expected. Calm, sophisticated and not given to the rituals of business deals. I told him about the Sea Lion and he didn't go through the jazz of pretending not to be interested.

He stuffed a cigarette into a long cane holder and then looked over at me as he leaned back.

'You speak very good German, Mr Farne. Was it the war?'

'Partly. Mainly a German mother.'

He nodded. 'Well, what's the deal?'

'I've got an option on her at thirty-five thousand dollars. It will take ten days to get her into shape. Say another thousand, and allow a couple of thousand for replacements, that brings her up to thirty-eight. I should want six on top of that so that's forty-four thousand. Have a year with her and if you're not happy I'll sell her for you next year at the same figure less my ten per cent.'

'What about a survey?'

'I always advise clients to have a survey. Protects us both. I'm not a qualified marine surveyor but I know boats. She's OK. You could take her out now but she doesn't look as good as she could.'

He stood up. 'Which would you prefer? Cash or irrevocable letter of credit?'

'Half-and-half would suit me.'

Twenty-two thousand dollars doesn't take up as much space as you'd think. Not even in hundred-dollar bills, but it's got a nice feel about it. There were big lobsters in the market and I bought a couple and a pile of peaches. As I headed for the boat I could see a crowd of men, twenty or more, looking down at her. And I knew there was something wrong. I couldn't actually recall closing the sea-cocks. The fishermen loved watching luxury cruisers in trouble. Especially when they sank. I knew what to expect. She was probably half under, held by one of the ropes so that she hung like a child's toy. Fire it wouldn't be, or they'd be doing something and shouting. They were absolutely silent. I pushed through the crowd and looked down at the boat. The tide had ebbed and the boat was about five feet below. There was no water slopping on the after-deck. But there was a sleeping girl. Topless and unaware of her silent admirers. Her head was pillowed on the folded sleeping bag and her fine blonde hair had blown across her face. One hand cradled her cheek and the other lay relaxed as she lay slightly turned to one side. The two big mounds of her breasts were quite naked and the spiky tips were the colour of tinned salmon. Despite the lovely face and the inviting body she wasn't just sexy. Even asleep there was a kind of indifference to being stared at. She must be used to it anyway. Like the others I looked for a moment, and then I turned and waved them off. *'Basta amici – andiamo,'* and they went off grinning with a few last lingering looks.

I loosened the warps and kept my eye on the stragglers and then went down the vertical ladder at the side of the quay.

She stirred slightly and I draped one of the big bath towels over her and she stretched like a cat and snuggled down.

I trailed a power cable up to the box on the jetty and

wired in a transformer because it was 110V. When I put the main switch on we'd got power and light all over the boat. I put the charger on to the first pair of batteries and unscrewed the caps. Then I pulled up the deck plates and got down to the engines. They were big inboard/outboards and I'd cleaned them and painted them at Chichester. I found the loose screw that held the pawl on the faulty lifting gear and finally switched on the bilge pump. The filter was clean and was soon gurgling as the last inch or so of oil and water was sucked out.

When I got back up in the cockpit madam had gone, but the doors to the saloon were latched back open. She was sitting at the saloon table drinking a Coke. I took her for a meal at the little restaurant by the church, and then we walked up the hill to where the olives started. It was just after ten when we got back.

I poured us both a whisky and lit a cigarette. Her chin was resting on the back of her hand and her big eyes were running a search party over my face. When they got to the grey thatch on top, she spoke.

'Are you married?'

'Nope.'

'Never?'

'Just once.'

'What happened?'

'When I got back from the war I found I'd provided one of the first GI brides.'

'Any children?'

'Not that I know of.'

'Have you always been in boats?'

'Pretty well. Tried cars once but I'm not sharp enough.'

'You *look* tough enough.'

'Tough and sharp's two different things, sweetie.'

'Where do you live apart from boats?'

'I live on a boat at Birdham Pool near Chichester.'

'Does it make you money?'

'Enough for me.'

She was twiddling the empty glass. A thing girls do, either because they want more or because they're going to tell you something on the lines of 'It's all over, Charlie' or both.

I tanked her up and waited. I hoped it wasn't going to be the story of her life because I'd decided that I'd rather have the other thing. I'd been a bit slow, a bit puritan, and I'd got so I regretted it. Mind you, if I'd known how it was going to end up, I'd have settled for just holding hands.

'D'you know when Pat's coming?'

'Pat. Who's Pat?'

'Pat Dixon.'

And the lightning struck. Pat Dixon was the rag-trade man. The owner of the boat. Or he would be when he traded his dough in a couple of days for the little blue book that made him the owner of 64/64, the good ship *Lucky Penny*. The man who had letters delivered to him by gunmen.

'You know him?'

She nodded.

'You his girlfriend?'

'Sort of.'

'What's that mean?'

'He's got several. I'm the Bohemian deb one.'

'And the others?'

'There's a twinset and pearls one, a huntin', shootin' and fishin' one, a rich bitch one and a boyhood romance one – she's Jewish. There may be more but I haven't heard of them.'

'That's why you came to this boat?'

She nodded. 'He said he'd booked us in at the Imperiale and in a couple of days we'd stay on the boat and cruise around for three or four weeks.'

'What happened at the Imperiale?'

'They said the booking had been cancelled two days ago. They couldn't help. Mr Dixon hadn't given them instructions about stray girls. The manager looked like he'd do a personal deal but I told him to shove it.'

'Well, he'll be here in a couple of days and then you can both sort it out. And if you don't, I'm taking a Chris Craft back with me and you can swab the decks or something.'

'I don't think he'll come.'

'He'll come all right, honey, he wants this boat.' And then I realized that it was one of those things that could have been better phrased. I topped her up again from the bottle.

'Honey, I'm going to check the mooring lines. It'll take me ten minutes to the second. I want you in your bunk by then. And if you're a good girl I'll make you an eggnog.'

There were tears brimming in her big grey eyes but I wasn't in the market. I turned smartly and cracked my head on the barometer as I went up the steps. I gave her fifteen minutes and went back in. There was a light on over the galley but the rest was darkness. I switched on the radio and tuned to the BBC. They were bashing out 'The Lady is a Tramp' and I moved down the dial to Radio 3. They were playing Massenet's 'Last Sleep of the Virgin'. It wasn't my night. I moved on to AFN and settled for Tommy Dorsey doing 'Getting Sentimental Over You'.

I whisked up an egg, dumped in some sugar and then the milk was frothing over the cooker. A slug of milk and another good whisk, a furtive aspirin, more frothy milk and it was done. A saucer and a biscuit and Nurse Farne was in action. A lot of blonde hair hung down the side of the bunk and her face was on the edge of the foam cushion.

'Here you are, honey. Makes you feel worse if you hang your head down. Have a drink of this.'

She hunched up on to an elbow and reached for the glass. There was no ignoring the two beautiful boobs. They were the size and smoothness of superior marker buoys. She obviously didn't mind my looking and I looked till she'd finished the drink. When she lay back on the pillows she didn't cover them up and there was a great urge on my part to help support them. But the therapy was to play at little girls being tucked up in bed so I pulled the duvet over her shoulders, kissed her ear and patted her bottom.

Out in the cockpit the tide had come in and the flat mahogany hand-rails were level with the quay. I stowed the gang-plank for the night and got the hoses out and sat smoking while both water tanks filled.

I wondered what Mr Pat Dixon was up to. He'd struck me as an exceptionally pleasant guy for the rag-trade. About thirty-five one of those lucky Jews who combine the two Jewish genetic patterns of shrewdness and creativeness. The clothes he sold were cheap, but they were bright and gay. *His* designs, *his* choice of cut and material and they filled a nice slice of the market. But there were no florid jokes about Jews and when I looked through his record racks while I was waiting for him there was a nice mixture from Bach to Vivaldi. There were some touches of vulgarity but we've all got those. The list of girlfriends didn't surprise me nor did their descriptions. But the casual indifference to Tammy's feelings did. I spend time weighing up clients. If they want the Eastern bazaar haggle bit I'll go along, but Dixon had asked a few questions, they weren't the right ones, so I answered them, and then told him the right ones. He'd laughed and wasn't offended and we didn't have to go through the pathetic ritual of a business deal. But if he and the blonde didn't square off, I'd be glad of her company on the way back. And I wouldn't be doing my Florence Nightingale act either.

Three

The next morning was one of those Italian mornings. At eight o'clock you could hear the noise of Lambrettas across the water from the town. The air was clear and you could see the girls on the tiny beach. The sky was a solid wash of blue and the heat, even at that early hour, made noises in your head. Deckhands were busy putting up awnings on the gin-palaces and there was a row of sparkling cars lining the mole.

There were three letters for me at the Post Office and I walked across the piazza to the Pensione di Ligure. The tables had been cleaned and the Birra umbrellas were up and I had a cappuccino while I looked through the mail. The first was a leaflet and sales pitch for a new range of marine radios extolling the virtues of single-side-band reception. They were right, but late in the day with their discovery. The second was from an old client who wanted to flog a Moonraker for a motor-sailer and would I take it on. The third was postmarked London and had taken five days to make the trip. Inside there was an irrevocable letter of credit for the price of *Lucky Penny*, a typewritten receipt for me to sign and return, and a handwritten letter from Dixon.

Dear Farne,
Hope you had a good trip.
  Flying direct to Milan tomorrow, will be with you Wednesday latest. Can't wait to take her over. Money enclosed. Did you insure with Newton Crum?
  Have booked in at Imperiale for a few days. Will you contact a Tammy Walton there? She'll be cruising with me. Tell Mario to let her have any cash she needs and I'll square up on arrival. Keep an eye on her.
  Don't forget local frequency crystal. All for now.
  Yours
  Pat Dixon.

I checked over the days and the dates again and it didn't make sense. If he'd arrived on the Wednesday, he would have been here the day before I came in. Selfish to the last I went across to the Banca di Roma and paid for a special clearance of the letter of credit. They phoned Rome and London and there was no hold-up. They offered me cash and I took it.

  The Imperiale wasn't joining in the Italian day. It was all cool, quiet and shade. The girl at reception checked her cards and confirmed that a two-room booking for Signor Dixon had been cancelled. No, she didn't know who cancelled or how or when. Only the Direttore would know. Signor Frascatti was all cool charm. Wondered why I was asking questions. Who I was. He gave me an expert going over with his big brown eyes and that didn't worry me. All my life, even when I've been broke, people have assumed that I'm filthy rich. Maybe it's the boats or maybe the tatty clothes. Or maybe it's just that the real function of wealth is the ability to say 'Get stuffed' when you feel so inclined. I had that ability but without the back-up.

I passed the test and he got up and walked over to a row of filing cabinets. He brought back a blue file cover and opened it. There were a dozen or so pieces of paper and he read through three or four at the top. He shook his head and looked up. 'We had a telephone call. From London. From Signor Dixon himself. Cancelling the two rooms. That's all I can tell you.' He closed the file.

'How did the hotel know it was Signor Dixon on the phone?'

He smiled and spread his hands. 'We don't know for sure, of course. But the cancellation of two rooms is not for us a big formality. Especially at this time of the year. It is not high season. If it was a joke or a mistake and Signor Dixon and his guest had arrived, we would have found them accommodation.'

When I got back to the boat the girl was sitting with Mario in the cockpit. The sleep had done her good. Mario got me a Pellegrini and some peanuts. I handed over the cash and told him to transfer it through his account to my Swiss account.

Mario had uncovered an American who wanted a particular boat. Must be that specific make because American-made was best. It wouldn't do to enlighten him that although it was well-made it was made in Hong

Kong. Mario had fixed for me to see him that evening at the Elena.

We were invited to eat that evening with Mario and his wife. Only I knew what a compliment that was. All the rich boys who saw Mario as the chap who ran errands for them would have been shocked if they had seen Signora del Bruna and their home. Mafalda del Bruna unmarried had been the Contessina di Pioli and the background was unmistakable. The villa on the edge of the town was run with smooth efficiency and a warmth of welcome that made it home for a wide variety of people.

When Mario had gone, I tackled the lobsters and it was an hour before we ate. The Chianti had made young Tammy talkative.

'Mario's a real fan of yours.'

'Great.'

'Says you're a really nice man.'

There's nothing worse than being labelled a 'nice' man by a pretty girl you've got designs on.

'I had a letter from Pat Dixon this morning.'

Her face got that look of waiting to hear teacher read out the 'O' level results.

'What did he say?'

'Here. Read it.'

And I turned back to do the washing-up. She was a lazy little bitch. She read the letter and then there was some silence.

'What d'you think's happened to him?'

'Why should something have happened to him? He just hasn't come, that's all.' I knew what she meant but I needed a check to see if it was more than feminine intuition stuff, which is often only one step removed from always expecting the worst.

'He would have kept you informed. Sent a telegram or something. You might have been planning to go back before now. And he's not like that.'

'Not like what?'

'Oh, indifferent to people. And the business at the hotel. He's not like that.'

I put the drying-cloth on the galley rack and sat down with her at the saloon table.

'So what do we do, Tammy?'

She laughed and shook her head. 'There's nothing much I can do. I haven't any money.'

'And if you had?'

'I'd try and find out from London if he left. If he did, I'd want to know more.'

'Right. We'll do that then.'

Mario treated us to the long-distance call and I spoke to Dixon's personal secretary. He had left as arranged. The accommodation at the Imperiale had not been cancelled by her or Dixon, and she had assumed that he was on his new boat at Santa Margherita. She would telephone Mario if she heard from Dixon.

I poured us both a drink when we got back to the boat just before midnight. I'd done a deal with the American so that was reason for a small celebration. Tammy started us off again.

'Why are we bothering about Pat?' She was looking pretty intently at me, waiting for my answer.

'Well, I never like losing a client in transit, and in your case I guess it's Auld Lang Syne or something.'

She shook her head. 'It's more than that. I think

something bad's happened. I think . . .' and her voice tailed off.

'You think what?'

'I think he's dead. You probably think I'm mad.'

'Not at all. The same thought's in my mind. I don't think he's dead, I think he could be. But thousands of people deliberately disappear every year for one reason or another. Or he could have met with an accident. By the way, do you know anyone around Dixon with the initials D.T.?'

She frowned and thought for a few moments. 'No, I don't. Not off-hand anyway. Why? What's that got to do with it?'

'That note that the fellow with the gun had in his pocket. It was for Dixon and it was signed D.T.'

'My God, what *is* going on?'

'I don't know, honey. But I'm going to find out.'

'What do you think we should do?'

'He'll be a week overdue tomorrow. Tomorrow we'll clean down the boat. If we've heard nothing by the evening, I'll ring the police. In London, that is.'

The big blue eyes looked slightly tearful again.

'How's your hand now?'

'Fine.'

By four in the afternoon the next day the boat looked new. Short of slipping her she was in prime condition. With Tammy scrubbing the decks we'd had plenty of offers of help. And never before in Santa Margherita had there been so many interested bystanders – not since Anita Ekberg was here anyway.

At four fifteen we sat, dirty but self-righteous in our

wet clothes, drinking long gin and lemonades. Nobody had mentioned Pat Dixon. There had been nothing in the post. So I dived in.

'Tell me about Pat Dixon, Tammy. What's he like?'

She wrinkled her nose and flicked back the heavy blonde hair and left her hand on her shoulder.

'It's hard to say. He seemed extrovert but there was a private part, a sort of backroom that he could retreat to and nobody got in there.'

'How'd you meet him?'

'I was at Goldsmith's and I won a prize that his company had offered for the design of a dress material.'

'When was this?'

'Just over a year ago.'

'How often did you see him?'

'Once or twice a week.'

'Weekends?'

'No, never. That was strictly taboo.'

'Any talk of marriage?'

She pulled a wry face and laughed.

'He never talked of it and I wouldn't have married him anyway.'

'Why not?'

'Nobody, but nobody, is ever going to be allowed in that backroom. He was a swinger and the parties and the trips would be great, but you've always got to come home sooner or later. It would always be his home and that part would be out of bounds.'

Little Tammy wasn't as dumb as she was blonde. Most women would have settled for the deal, given the chance.

'I imagine he was an attractive man?'

She sipped her drink and then looked up with a half-smile.

'Yes, I slept with him – which is where you were heading for.'

'A normal sort of guy?'

She shook her head.

'No.'

'In what way not?'

The big grey eyes weighed me up as she hesitated. She looked down at her empty glass.

'He'd never do it more than once. And it was like it was a favour. A favour to me, that is.'

I thought about that for a couple of minutes but it rang no useful bells. With all those girlfriends, maybe he had a rationing system.

'How about we get you some clothes, Tammy, and we'll nip into Rapallo for a meal tonight?'

'The shops will be closed, won't they?'

'We'll go to La Roba. The old dragon who runs it owes me a favour or two.'

I went mad and bought her a denim safari suit, a couple of dresses and a heap of oddments, but best of all was an emerald linen dress with a short skirt. Tammy in the green dress spoiled the evening for a lot of ladies in Rapallo. And she made mine when she gave a po-faced shake of the head to a couple of swingers who came over bowing and scraping for a dance. And the orchestra obliged with my request for an old song from 1943. Somebody's old dad hummed it for them. It was the Italian version of 'Dearly Beloved' – *'Un sol' amore e questo sei tu . . .'*

While she was powdering her nose, I phoned Mario.

The taxi dropped us by the fish market. It was a lovely calm, peaceful night, and she hooked her arm in mine and hummed to herself as we walked. Nothing romantic, mind you – just the 'Wombles of Wimbledon', but I knew it was well meant.

We sat in the saloon with a whisky apiece and I told her when I was pouring a refill, 'Tammy, I'm going to London for a couple of days. I've fixed for you to stay with Mario and his wife while I'm away. Is that OK with you?'

She nodded, but looked very young, as though she were being sent to bed early.

I was zipping the sleeping bag when she came out. She was beautifully naked. The fairy off the top of the Christmas tree. There was nothing to say, but that didn't stop her from saying it. She knelt down beside me on the deck. 'I'll miss you while you're away.' I kissed her long but gently and unzipped the bag with my one good hand. It was two hours later when I came up for air. She was wrapped around me but I sat and looked up at the stars. There were two yellow eyes about four feet up from mine on the quayside. I froze, and then relaxed. It was a cat. It sat there with its prim paws together, its head pushed forward to see better and it looked shocked and bemused. It must have been there some time.

Four

The plane was in the Heathrow box and, as we swung over the Thames at the Houses of Parliament, London looked at its best. A long way away. London, early on a Sunday morning with few people and no cars, was the only London I cared for. The rest of the time it seemed an old rotten log, crawling with soft slugs and hard-cased beetles. The boat at Chichester gave me complete independence. No mortgages, no rates, no lawns to mow, no commuter journey, no grim-faced fellow humans pouring out of holes in the ground to find their daily bread. Part of me could have been happy with a wife and family, but not in a town and earning a routine living. And it's a woman in a million who'd spend her married life on a boat. And I'd only met a few thousand. I had independence, low-cost living, complete freedom to follow the sun and all the pretty girls a man could want.

The galley was the best money could buy and Westinghouse could make. The stereo hi-fi and 400 cassettes supplied my music, and the old polished mahogany was as gentle on the soul as candlelight on the eye. I didn't live rough and I'd never need to. And I hadn't had even a cold in twenty-five years. I was out of the UK 250 days a year so I didn't pay tax. Anywhere. I didn't do much that was illegal, and what I did in that direction was fair when it broke a stupid rule. There was a touch of piracy, but only against the big boys.

I reckoned I could afford to give three weeks to finding Dixon – dead or alive. The boat money was in my bank but the boat was still mine. Until that blue book was transferred I owned her and, as it said on her documents, 'her guns, ammunition and appurtenances'. I'd need a few days snooping around in London, Tammy would be safe with Mario, and a bit of mothering would do her morale a lot of good.

We came down fast and the traffic on the M4 was thick, like a big display of Dinky Toys. I'd booked a room at the Special Forces Club; I left my bag in the hall and got a taxi to Brook Mews where Dixon had his offices and flat.

His personal assistant found she could spare me a few minutes. Miss Lakeman-Hart was a cool Swedish-type blonde, and I marked her down as the twinset and pearls girlfriend. Her legs were a bit on the thin side but her face would have turned on Prince Rainier. It was a later model but the same architect. She was so calm that you wanted to close your eyes and go to sleep. It must be pretty difficult to be that beautiful and not have even one gramme of sexiness. It would be like bedding down with one of the wax models from Madame Tussaud's.

She sat with her legs crossed and the good tweed

skirt right to her knees. Her right hand touched the pearls for reassurance but she didn't really need it.

'But if you've been paid, Mr Farne, I don't quite see what you want.'

'I'm concerned about Mr Dixon. I want to check on where he is.'

She drew herself up and her back was straight like they taught her at Roedean. She frowned, and sacrificed the smooth skin of her forehead. Her blue eyes were big with contrived amazement.

'But really, Mr Farne, I can't see that it's any of your business what Mr Dixon does.'

'Is it yours?'

'Of course.'

'Well, what have you done about it?'

'Mr Dixon frequently makes trips without informing us where he is going.'

'But he did say where he was going. And he didn't go there. He's now ten days overdue. Is that typical?'

'I couldn't discuss my boss's business with you, Mr Farne.'

'It's that or you discuss it with the police.'

There was a thin look about her mouth and I guessed Pat Dixon hadn't done it with her more than once at a time either.

'What on earth has it got to do with the police?'

'They're responsible for missing persons, Miss Hart.'

Miss Lakeman-Hart stood up and brushed some imaginary crumbs from her skirt. Then she folded her arms across her chest and said, 'I think Mr Dixon would want you to respect his privacy, Mr Farne. That's the advice I would give you.' She might as well have said outright 'the likes of you', but she was just a bit uneasy.

The boyhood sweetheart lived with her family in one of the post-war estates at the back of Gants Hill. It was a semidetached house covered with spec builders' stucco.

Rosa Meyer was a honey. Dark-complexioned, long black hair and only a swine like me would have noticed the full breasts and the long legs. If the Jews had royalty, she would be a princess. There were pink mirrors, garish wallpaper, solid furniture and plastic flowers, but if my name had been Marks or Spencer I'd have been hanging round there every night. Her family and Dixon's family had been friends for years when they both lived in Aldgate, and she'd smilingly told me that it was still their greatest wish that the two should marry.

'And will you?'

She shook her head. 'No. We should be most unsuitable.'

'In what way?'

'He has many qualities and many talents. Good-looking, good company and very likeable. But he's not a serious man.'

'In what way?'

She held her head on one side as she thought and her voice was very gentle as she spoke.

'It's not easy to explain but there's a phrase in the Bible that people always misquote. They say, "Money is the root of all evil". It doesn't say that at all; it says "*Love* of money is the root of all evil". My father has a small company in Aldgate making shirts. He makes

34

money, but he could make much more if he hadn't spent so much time with my mother and us girls. He cares about money but he *loves* us. Pat Dixon loves money and power and he'll never love a woman like that. I don't know which came first, the not loving a woman or the loving of money.'

'But your father would like you to marry him?'

'I'm a kind of alibi for Pat Dixon. Looking like he'd like to marry me saves a lot of questions.'

'What sort of questions?'

'Where he's going, where he's at, all the questions that some men never want to answer. They don't want to know themselves. Keep moving and you don't have to look in the mirror.'

I would have liked Rosa Meyer as a friend for life, but I would have ended up wanting more than friendship and instinct told me I wouldn't get it. But I liked her enough to tell her what had happened. She was silent for a time and then she looked at me as though I mattered.

'I should be very careful.'

'Careful of what?'

She rubbed a lovely ankle as she sorted out what to say.

'I think Pat Dixon is a dangerous man.'

'But you said he was likeable.'

She smiled. 'Many women find dangerous men likeable. Criminals are loved by their wives and children. But criminals never love back. They're sentimental and that's all. To them people are objects not persons.'

She was plaiting her hair as if I wasn't there and I knew that it was time to go.

'What do you do, Rosa? Work, I mean.'

She smiled. 'Guess.'

I didn't hurry, and it gave me a good excuse to look her over again. Oh how I wished I'd been a Bar Mitzvah boy. But there wasn't a clue.

'I give up.'

She laughed. 'I'm a probation officer.'

I got up and she shook hands still smiling.

'Could I come again if I need help?'

She held my hand in hers and then gently put her other hand there too. I hoped it wasn't just some old Jewish custom. Then she kissed me gently and said, 'Of course,' I felt like asking for fourteen previous offences to be taken into consideration.

There are only two places in London you can get a real John Collins and one is the Special Forces Club. I had one as a nightcap and anything less suitable I can't imagine. But my brain was fuddled with London and questions and answers. The big diesels were thudding between my ears again. But one thing was for sure. I was going to find Dixon. Dead or alive.

I hired a Capri the next morning and with a couple of wrong turns got myself down to Woldingham just before eleven. 'Four Winds' was all Moorish, Bauschule and Odeon but it stood back in at least five acres. I'd phoned from London and milady was expecting me. This was the rich bitch girlfriend. She was about five feet five and very thin. I'm not too sure what's silk and what's shantung but the black dress was one or the other. It hung well except that she had no bust and that made her nipples look like press-studs as the thin material clung to her. There were no bells on her toes but there were rings on her fingers. My God, there were rings. And they flashed, sparkled and exploded as she waved her very fine, slender hands. She smoothed everything before she sat down and then waited patiently, head back slightly, for the news from Ghent. I gave her only the barest details.

'Oh, my dear, what will the silly man do next. Are you worried about him, Mr . . . er, Farne?'

'Concerned. How about you?'

She frowned. All Dixon's women seemed to do a lot of frowning. But Veronica Page used it to show deep thoughts.

'Well, he does go out of circulation from time to time, you know. But never more than a couple of days. One says nothing and draws one's own conclusions.'

And we smiled together like the knowing bastards we were.

'What conclusions have you drawn?'

'It's those girls. I don't know what he sees in them. He's far more at home down here.'

'What sort of man is he?'

'Fantastic talent, a great personality. In the right hands, he could get right to the top.'

And in case I hadn't rumbled which were the right hands she spread them in Gallic appeal.

'After I put the cash up in the early days he's never looked back. But he mixes with too many wrong people, you know.'

'The girls, you mean?'

'Not just them but the waifs and strays he picks up.'

'What sort of waifs and strays?'

37

'Oh, odd little men. I went to Pat's place one night – by arrangement, I might emphasize – and he was sitting with this man drinking. Appalling clothes, cockney accent, belched every two minutes while swigging beer and eyeing me up and down as if I were some tart. And he spoke to Pat as if he was giving the orders. And last time I saw Pat – about three weeks ago, that ghastly Mavis woman was there and a foreigner. Ugh. An Italian or something. What's that other part down the bottom?'

'Calabria?'

'No, no. An island.'

'Sicily?'

'That's it, and Mavis and the little man went off when I arrived. Pat didn't even introduce us. Must have felt thoroughly ashamed. Didn't want to talk about them but I told him exactly what I thought.'

'What was that?'

'He shouldn't be seen with such people. Said it was work, not pleasure, and shut me up.'

She looked at the diamond-heavy watch and I took the hint.

Mavis Trevor had a farm near Penshurst in Kent. She was inspecting a horse in the yard by the stable block when I arrived, and after a brief glance at me and a nod she carried right on. When she had finished she gave some instructions to the girl holding the horse and turned to face me, hands on hips. One thing was for sure: this wasn't one of Dixon's girlfriends. Her eyes were hard and experienced, and not all the experiences had been good. She didn't examine my teeth but her mouth made it clear that she would have sent me to the knacker's yard if it had been up to her.

'Well, what can I do for you, Mister?'

I explained the basic details about Pat Dixon and her face showed no surprise, no interest and no curiosity.

'And why come down here?'

'I thought you might be able to help.'

'Why?'

'I gather you're a friend of his.'

'And who said that?'

'Tammy. Tammy Walton.'

'And where'd you meet up with her?'

'In Santa Margherita.'

Her eyes flickered for a moment and then she looked down as her foot idly rolled a stone while she thought things over.

'Well, I can't help you,' and she looked at me with a challenging look. So I challenged her back.

'I think you can, Miss Trevor.'

She rocked gently on her feet as men do when considering aggression. So I went on very tentatively fishing.

'I'm just checking that none of his friends know where he is before I go to the police.'

Her chin went up slightly. 'Probably with one of those little floozies.'

I shook my head and turned as if to go. 'No, Miss Trevor, it's more than that and it's time somebody official was told,' and I put my hand out to shake hers. There were two spots of red on her cheeks.

'You'd better have a cup of tea before you go back to town.'

She pumped me hard over the cup of tea. What police,

would it be Albany Street? Who else had I contacted? What did they think? How did I know he hadn't just changed his mind about going to the boat? From indifference to keen interest but only because of the mention of the police.

'Did he come here often, Miss Trevor?'

'Not more than once a month.'

'What sort of man was he?'

'I really know very little about him.'

'A business friend?'

'No, not at all – an acquaintance more.' We could have been talking about a leper.

'But he liked the countryside.'

'We had mutual friends, that is all.'

As I drove slowly back to London I thought about Pat Dixon's girlfriends and their comments. Not exactly a fan club. I stopped at Sevenoaks and telephoned Veronica Page.

'Farne, Miss Page. Something I forgot to ask.'

'Oh yes?'

'How much money did you put up for Pat Dixon when he started?'

'A bit naughty you asking me that. But I suppose it doesn't matter really. It was ten thousand.'

'Did you put any more in after that?'

There was a long silence at the other end and then she spoke slowly, 'What made you ask that?'

'I thought he might have asked you for more recently. Say a month ago.'

She almost whispered, 'How on earth did you find out?'

'I didn't, Miss Page. I just wondered.'

'He asked me for a lot of money but I didn't give it to him.'

'How much did he want?'

'A hundred thousand.'

'For the business?'

'So he said.'

'Why did you refuse?'

'I felt there was something wrong somewhere.'

'In the business?'

'Yes. But there were no real grounds for thinking that.'

'Did he say why he wanted it?'

'To expand.'

I hesitated and then decided to plunge. It was easier on the phone. 'Miss Page, forgive me for asking you this, but did you check up on him or the business before you refused?'

She sighed. 'Yes, I got my accountant to do it.'

'What did he report?'

'Said Pat was up to something. Was in trouble and I shouldn't get mixed up in it.'

'Did you tell Dixon this?'

'No. I made an excuse. Said the money was tied up. He knew better than that, though.'

'What did he say?'

'He was terribly upset. Pleaded with me. Offered me a partnership and . . .' She trailed off.

'And asked you to marry him?'

'Yes, my God, and now he's gone. Do you think he's done something silly?'

'Not what you mean, Miss Page. Thanks for your help.'

She was crying as she hung up and I liked her for that. She'd recovered when I got back to the Club and phoned her for the name of her accountant.

George Henry Snelgrove would have preferred not to speak to me at all, but when a client such as Veronica Page gave you the nod it was not to be ignored. But he fought a hand to hand battle to avoid giving me an inch that I hadn't won. He had a file open on his desk and he referred to it from time to time.

'It was a private company, Mr Farne, so the liabilities were personal.'

'Who were the shareholders?'

'My client, Mr Dixon himself and a Mavis Trevor.'

'Had anybody got their investment back?'

'Dividends had been paid which were in excess of the initial investments.'

'And in recent years?'

'No dividend last year and this year's accounts are not yet issued.'

'Any indications?'

'From my enquiries there would have been a substantial loss but the company would still be solvent and capable of trading.'

'Was Dixon in trouble?'

'Financial trouble, you mean?'

'No, any trouble.'

He didn't like this at all. Yes or no answers were OK but like 'Twenty Questions' you mustn't just fish.

'Mr Farne, the laws of libel and slander in this country are a goldmine for the unscrupulous, so you will understand my caution about Mr Dixon. Let me say that I

42

can see no justification for Mr Dixon to require large sums of money for his business. It was not doing well but it did not need money, it needed management. Equally, in looking back through the accounts, I wonder if the current results are not normal and the previous results the exception. At the present poor trading level the shareholders are getting ten per cent on an invest-ment that has been returned already many times over. More than that, I am not prepared to say.'

Johnny Haynes, also ex-SOE, did his training on the same course as me. While others studied at night we headed for the nearest Palais de Danse. Superintendent J.A. Haynes didn't look all that much different. The pug face still grinned amiably and the shrewd eyes were still the same. He sucked his teeth while I made my request.

'Christ, Max. I can't give you a shufti at some villain's CRO file even if he did have a go at you. Anyway, I've sent a précis to the Italian police. Try them.'

'How about you have a look and then we just chat for a bit?'

He shook his head but he reached for the phone.

'Sergeant Ames? Right. I want the CRO file on Montague C. Dodds. The one we extracted for the Santa Margherita police. I don't want the alias cards but there is an entry on the Wanted Persons Index still outstanding. I'll have that and the Criminal Route Map . . . Fine. Quick as you can.'

We talked about old mates for five minutes and then he had the thick files in front of him. He read a few random pages and then looked up.

'I'll give you bits from his "Cemotstatt". That do you?'

I nodded and he went to the back of the file and read silently for several minutes. 'Cemotstatt' is the mnemonic the police use to cover the ten salient points of a criminal's M.O. It doesn't cover specific crimes, just the pattern, the method of operating.

Then he looked up. 'You ready?'

'Yes.'

'Classword: banks, large houses, industrial pay clerks. Entry: forcible with weapons. Means: part of gang. Object: personal gain, lately malice. Time: pay days, weekends, occupiers asleep. Style: not applicable. Tale: not applicable. Accomplice: list of fourteen names in twelve years. All except one on CRO files. The one exception dead. Transport: not applicable. Trade mark: killed guard dogs, used violence even when victims co-operative.'

He leaned back. 'He'll make a lovely corpse. Any other items?'

'What sort of hold-ups were they, Johnny?'

He pursed his lips in feigned reluctance.

'Big payrolls, banks, jewels and stuff from big houses. He was much in demand as a heavy. Then he moved out suddenly about six months ago. He was the heavy on the gang who did the factory at Croydon. A constable was killed. Dodds probably went to Spain. Most likely ended up doing little contracts on the continent. Harassment of debtors. Administration of Justice Act 1970, section forty stuff.'

'Anyone on the list of associates with the initials D.T.?'

He sighed and opened the file again and silently read down the list. Then he shook his head.

'No, Max. No surname with a T at all.'

'Thanks.'

'The DPP sent details to the Italians of our courts' attitude on non-criminal homicide. Quoted *Palmer v Regina* 1971 amongst others. Looks like they'll accept self-defence despite failure to retreat. Bear that in mind. They didn't seem all that worried.'

'Buy you a lunch?'

'Thanks, no. I'm due leave tomorrow and I must get the pile down a bit. Let me know how it goes.'

There was a night charter flight from Gatwick and they slipped me in. We landed at Milan and I took the airport bus to the station. The main station at Milan was like a cool cathedral and I had time for a coffee before I caught the train. It was almost six o'clock when I got out at Santa Margherita. I walked down the steps to the via Pagani and along the promenade. It was so wonderful to be back in Italy. I didn't kiss the earth but if anyone had insisted I shouldn't have hesitated. Even in the early morning light the fronts of the houses glowed with amber and russet warmth. By the time I got to the Banca di Roma the sun was through and the shadows were sharp and black, and the mist that swirled in from the bay was slowly curling and melting. By the end of the promenade you could see the misty shapes of the boats. The sea was flat and still and already there was no green, just the reflection of the cloudless sky in cerulean blue.

I'd decided to sleep on the boat until midday. I'd see

Tammy later in the day. I wanted some time to myself. Somebody had put up the canvas hood and I unclipped the press studs and stepped down into the cockpit. The saloon doors were locked and I took the spare key from under the echo-sounder. The air in the saloon was clean and fresh. The carpet was turned back and the cabin sole boards had been lifted to give a flow of air. The starboard windows were slightly open. Everywhere was polished and clean and it all looked very shipshape. I turned on the radio and it was one of the quieter of Tartini's 150 violin sonatas, pleasantly cheating with a piano instead of a harpsichord. All around was the actual warmth as well as the spiritual warmth of Italy. I contemplated becoming a Catholic but decided on a cup of tea instead. Sipping the tea, I knew I was dog-tired but I was taking a long time to get my head down. Stretched out on the big triangular for'ard bunk, I knew in the few moments before my eyes closed what was the matter. I wished that Tammy was there. I wished she'd been waiting at the airport when I got off the plane. There was a price for living my sort of life and this was part of the payment. Every now and then you get just a little bit lonely.

Five

I reported my return to the *questura* but nobody seemed all that excited. I asked the Tenente if they had found where Dodds came from. He was a big dark Sicilian and he chopped off the ends of his words, even when he spoke in English.

'He can' from Milan'. Before then Basel an' before then Cost' de Sol. He wanting by Swiss and French police for murder an' damage to persons. You forget, eh. There be no troubles.'

'Who was he working for?'

He shook his head. 'Not *nessuno* in Italia.'

I phoned Mario from the Bar Sole and I read through yesterday's *Corriere della Sera* while I was waiting. Inflation was to be 'regulated' down to a mere 21%. A starlet from Cine Città gave her views on divorce. There were complaints about the lifestyle of immigrant workers from the south. And a scathing review of a visiting company's performance of *L'Italiana in Algeri* at La Scala.

'*Buon giorno*, Max. *Come stai?*' Mario threw his hat on the spare seat and sat down.

'How're things with you, Mario?'

'Oh, she's fine. Mafalda like her very much. She good girl.'

'Any business around?'

'Yes. An English who wants a big boat.'

'You think he'd go for the van Lent with the steel hull?'

'Is possible.'

'What does he do?'

'You say a merchant banker, yes? He got money in plastics fabricca in Torino.'

'Where's he staying?'

'The Miramare.'

'Let's go see him.'

Arthur Hughes was a dapper little man. Grey hair with a military moustache and walnut-brown eyes. And I gave him the run down on the van Lent. Fifty-eight foot overall. Twin Volvo Penta Diesels and all the rest of it.

'A maximum of eleven knots doesn't seem very fast.'

'Well, if it's speed you want, Mr Hughes, this isn't the boat. But over that speed and you're going to lose all the comforts. We'd be looking for a planing boat. It'll get you there quicker but she'll bang you around.'

'I see. But say just a little faster, how about that?'

'Well, if you're cruising, which you had in mind, you're really concerned with speed against tide and wind. Eleven knots will give you ample speed in these waters, and all round the French and English coasts. Go up five knots and you pay a lot more and you cut down your cruising range. The van Lent gives you a cruising range of 658 miles, you know.'

I could see his better judgement fighting with status. But I guessed he'd rather be shrewd than flashy.

'I've got much faster boats if you really want one, but this one's a real boat. She was owned by a very wealthy Greek when I bought her.'

'And how much is she going to cost me?'

'To buy or to run?'

'Both.'

'I paid nineteen thousand for her. Pounds that is. I've paid for both engines to be overhauled. All new instruments – Brookes and Gatehouse. She's had a thorough check by me. I'd want twenty-five for her and I'd throw in a pontoon mooring till the end of the season.'

'Let's say twenty-four thousand if I like her.'

'OK, but without the mooring.'

He looked across at Mario. 'Can you fix me a mooring?'

'This season, no. Next season, yes. I can fix you this season at Camogli or Chiavari.'

Hughes laughed and stood up.

'When can I see her?'

'I'll take you over this afternoon; she's lying at Rapallo. If you want her, we'll bring her back.'

I arranged with Mario for a two-man team to clean up the German's Sea Lion, and laid on a taxi for the afternoon. I sent a message to Tammy that she could join us on the boat trip if she wanted to. For some reason I felt uneasy about meeting her again; it would be easier with other people around. I stocked up with groceries and fruit and a few bottles of Soave and Valpolicella.

It was noon and inside the boat it was shaded but hot. I uncorked one of the bottles of Soave, poured a glass and sat down with a pad to make some notes. There was a pattern somewhere about Dixon and I couldn't get hold of it. Maybe writing it all down would help. I'd hardly started when the boat rocked gently and then again and, as I turned, Tammy was framed in the open doorway. She was smiling, with her golden hair backlit by the sun, and wearing her blue denim suit. As I stood up she came down the companionway and I looked at her lovely face before I kissed her. Under the jacket she was naked and as my hands closed over her breasts it was better than being met at the airport. She stood patiently as my fingers kneaded the firm flesh. When my hand went to the zip on the tight pants she took over, and as she stepped out of the heap of blue denim at her feet she kissed me with that full soft mouth as my hand moved between her legs. I couldn't wait for the comfort of the bunk; I wanted her then and there and she knew it and accommodated my lust as best she could. The second time, on the bunk, it was just as urgent, and when I'd finished she put her hands on my face and kissed me gently. 'Hello, Max. You're back,' and suddenly we were laughing. I got us two Cokes and we lay on the bunk together and I told her what had happened on my trip. I was up on one elbow with my Coke tin on her flat young belly and she said, 'You're not listening, Max.'

'I am.'

'If you want to look at me, say so.'

'I want to.'

She smiled as she opened her legs.

*   *   *

50

We were washed and brushed and presentable when the taxi hooted and in half an hour we were all on the quayside at Rapallo.

The van Lent was anchored well out and one of the fishermen rowed us out. I took off the covers and then they all came aboard. She was built in 1958 and was roomy and good-looking. I'd have liked another eighteen inches on the beam, but she sat well in the water and only drew five feet. A well-laid-out galley in teak and stainless steel, radio telephone and echo-sounder and, last but not least, the Sharps autopilot. A waste of money for trotting around the coast, but beginners always loved them. I took him down to the engine compartment and switched on the light. I made him put his hand on the big Pentas so that he knew they hadn't been warmed up. When he pressed the red button, they lumbered and thumped for a moment and then settled down to a good solid rhythm.

The boat was stern-on to the town. I pressed the winch button and the anchor came up sluggishly and I clamped her into place on the seating. I put Hughes at the wheel and went aft and hoisted up the stern anchor. She drifted slowly with the ebbing tide and back in the wheelhouse I put her into gear and turned her head till she faced the bay. After ten minutes there was a nice little lift as she cut through the swell. She was a good, solid, safe boat, and I knew she was right for Hughes. I let him take the wheel and bring her in a wide arc towards Santa Margherita, and as Rapallo disappeared in the slight early evening haze he said he'd take her. I radioed back to the harbourmaster at Rapallo and asked him to give a message to the taxi driver. When we came into the bay at Santa Margherita I got my scratch crew working, and showed Hughes the most important thing a boat man needs to know – how to keep the boat still, in one spot, against tide and wind and current. The GRP dinghy was already on the davits and she came down nicely; I took her line and brought her to the opening in the guard rails.

We all had a drink on my boat and I transferred one of my reserve moorings to the new owner. We were to meet at the Banca di Roma at ten the next morning, when I should be paid.

We had dinner that evening with Hughes and his family at the Miramare, and afterwards I walked Tammy to the main square, past the broken bridge and up to the point where the villas gave up the struggle and the olives and peaches took over. The town itself was in the dead ground below us, but out beyond the boats shone in the moonlight, and the lights from decks and port-holes sent golden ladders down the water. The air was filled with the scent of mimosa and the ground was still warm where we sat. In one of the gardens below, a nightingale sang and was challenged by another nearby. From one of the villas came the strains of an old Italian song from the war – '*Vento, vento portami via con te . . .*' and I sang it softly to the girl. It had taken first prize at the Naples Piedigrotta in 1942 and we'd used it as a partisan code. I'd sat on hillsides then, but the smell was of oil on gun barrels and in the silence we heard no nightingales. A loosened stone rolling was what set our hearts beating and more often than not there was snow. I loved the people then, but hated the country.

Now I loved it all. Crossing the border was like sliding tired into a warm, familiar bed.

Tammy's face was turned up to the deep blue sky and the stars, and the moonlight softened her glowing skin to magnolia.

'Tammy, I'll have to go back to London.'

'When?'

'Tomorrow, if I can get a plane.'

Her head came slowly down and rested on her drawn-up knees. She turned her face to look at me.

'Would you like to come with me? You can stay on my boat or with Mario if you want.'

'How long will you be gone?'

'A week, ten days, I'm not sure.'

'Is Pat Dixon dead?'

'I think so.'

'Do you know why and how?'

'I think I know why and I'm going to find out how.'

'I'd like to come with you.'

I kissed her and she responded eagerly. It was nearly midnight when we got back to the boat.

I gave Mario a long list of instructions about the various boats, Hughes' letter of credit for transfer, and a cheque for his commission and my expenses. He wouldn't take anything for Tammy's stay.

We were booked on a Pan-Am flight at six o'clock from Milan. It was nearly ten when I booked us in at the Hilton.

In the morning I bought the Ordnance Survey maps covering Penshurst and two four-inch-to-the-mile versions covering the farm. Then I went round to

Dixon's place. Miss Lakeman-Hart was on the phone as I went in. She recognized me immediately and put the phone down quickly.

'What can I do for you, Mr Farne?'

The phone rang. Somebody wanted to know why she'd hung up on them. She lifted the phone but kept her eyes on me.

'Hello. No, I'm afraid not. Please ring later.' And she hung up again.

'Any news of Mr Dixon?'

'I'm afraid not.'

'Who's running the business now?'

'Miss Trevor and I are looking after things.'

'What have you done about finding Mr Dixon?'

There were two red spots of anger on what was a very lovely face.

'Mr Farne, I must ask you to leave.'

'OK. May I use your phone?'

She waved her hand expansively in the direction of the phone. I picked it up and dialled.

'Hello. Is that Scotland Yard? Yes, please. Can you tell me how I get in touch with the Fraud Squad . . .'

One delicate finger had pressed down the bar and cut off the call. I leaned against the wall and looked at Miss Lakeman-Hart. Her calm, lovely face was flushed, and she didn't know what to do next. She was wearing a white silk shirt and a well-cut black skirt with a wide, shiny belt around her narrow waist. She was a very pretty girl and as I looked her over I wondered what had happened to the sex bit. Was it never there or did it go because of something that happened? She was obviously aware that I was looking

her over. She was the kind that could slap your face
for less. There was a little triangular block on her big
executive desk and it said 'Miss Daphne Lakeman-
Hart'. I smiled at her as I spoke.

'That was a silly thing to do, Daphne.'

By then she'd looked me over too and decided she
did know what to do. She leaned casually against the
filing cabinet, her body arched so that I got a grand-
stand view of what was in the white shirt. They weren't
in the same class as Tammy's but there was quite a lot
of girl in there. When I looked back at her face she
was smiling and she looked almost inviting.

'I think we'd better have a talk, Mr Farne,' and she
nodded towards the open door of Dixon's big office.
The wall-to-wall was rather like the yielding turf of
Wembley Stadium that gave Cup Finalists the cramps.
There were two or three massive armchairs and a wide,
curving settee that would hold six or seven people with
room to spare. There was a big low circular glass table
in front of the settee. The girl had gone over to a drinks
cabinet and was fiddling about with glasses. Her back
had a kind of guilty look and I wondered if she had in
mind slipping me a Mickey Finn. She walked over, put
down the drinks and then sat down beside me on the
soft leather settee. I sipped the long drink. It was a gin
and lime. Tasted normal and I turned to congratulate
her. Then I saw the reason for the fiddling about. She'd
undone the top two pearly buttons on her white shirt
and the goodies were on show. The black skirt was
halfway up her thighs and her long thin legs swept
down to fine ankles and black court shoes with diamanté
buckles. When my eyes had finished the grand tour, I

looked back at her face. Her big blue eyes looked into mine and her wide mouth was slightly open as she chinked her glass idly against her bottom teeth. She put her glass on the table and leaned towards me, putting one slim hand on my knee.

'What do you think's happened to Pat, Mr Farne?'

Never selfish or mean-spirited, I leaned towards her and put my hand on *her* knee.

'I think he's dead, Daphne,' and I moved my hand up her smooth nylon leg so that it was just under her skirt. She didn't react to the news or the hand, but looked at me thoughtfully as my hand stroked the warmth of her leg.

'What do you think happened to him?'

Her face was very near mine and it would have been rude not to kiss the pretty mouth. Somebody somewhere had pressed the defrosting button and the mouth responded eagerly. I loosened the other buttons and she gasped as my hand explored her breasts. She sighed as I pushed her back on the cushions. I slid the shirt from her shoulders and when I unzipped her skirt she helped me slide it down her long legs. She was wearing nylons and a white suspender belt. She watched my face as I looked at her body. Her thick blonde hair spread across the cushions and as I leaned over to kiss her she pulled me to her and her hand made me welcome down between her legs. When I'd done it to her twice, she stroked my face as I lay on her, and said softly, 'Was it good, Max? Was that what you wanted?' I said the appropriate things. She *was* a bitch. Only bitches ask that question, because to them it's all one-sided. They allow, they don't join the party. Then, still stroking my face, she said, 'Tell me what you think's happened to Pat,' and she moved under me to indicate the pay-off.

'I think he got himself into something he couldn't handle.' And I realized she'd called me Max. I hadn't given my name but maybe she'd looked at Dixon's notes on the boat deal. Her body still moved gently to remind me of forthcoming attractions and she didn't whisper. 'Tell me what it's all about, Max. What's he been up to?' But she'd moved once too often and I took over. I made it last a long time and, when I was at the point of no return, I heard her say, 'Oh God', and she struggled to get away. I held her shoulders till the music stopped. I looked up at her face. It was white and she was staring over my shoulder as she struggled to stand up.

In the doorway was Mavis Trevor. Her eyes blazed and the words tumbled over each other as she hissed, 'You filthy little bitch. You scum. You . . .' She ran out of words. She must have watched the last part of the performance and didn't think much of it. She stood and watched as we assembled ourselves again and I gave our Daphne a peck and said, 'I'll phone you later, sweetie.'

I'm sorry to say that despite my excitement something else had passed through my mind while I was enjoying my investigations. I phoned Johnny Haynes.

'Johnny, did Dodds have any relatives? Next of kin and so on?'

'Yeah. A wife and two grown-up kids.'

'Where do they live?'

'Can't remember. Hang on, I'll check.'

He was away for some time and then I heard the rustle of papers.

'Here we are. Wife Maureen. Lives at 42 Sheet Lane, South Croydon. Lived there fifteen years. D'you want the kids' addresses too?'

'No, that's fine, Johnny. Thanks.'

Sheet Lane probably was a lane sixty years ago, but now it was one of those dreary little streets that infect all the London suburbs. The houses were early Victorian but some occupiers had made gallant attempts at taking the advice in the Sunday supplements. Number 42 had a heavy panelled front door painted bright yellow. The treads of the sandstone steps were worn to a concave uniformity and when I pressed the button I knew it would be chimes. The woman who answered the door was small and perky. I said I'd called about Monty and she looked doubtful but let me in.

We went in the ceremonial front room. The smart boys would get plenty of laughs out of Mrs Dodds' front room, but I was brought up with one like that and I was at home. She smoothed her apron as she sat down and then realized where she was and untied it, folded it and sat on it.

'Did you know our Monty then?'

'Not very well, Mrs Dodds. I wondered how you were managing.'

'Were you one of his . . . er . . . business friends?'

'Not really. I only met him once.'

Her shrewd eyes didn't miss anything.

'You're a reporter, aren't you?'

'No. I just wanted to check that you were getting by.'

She nodded approvingly but she wasn't giving

anything away. 'I'm all right, dear, thank you. Would you like a cuppa before you go?'

It was done very nicely and I went. The heavy iron gate groaned as I closed it behind me. I wished then I hadn't needed to go.

We got a car from Avis and we were at Penshurst village exactly at midnight. There were no lights anywhere and I drove slowly towards the Hever Road. Half a mile from the farm I turned the car into a rutted track that ended just inside an open field gate. We walked up the lane till we could see the black outline of the farm and its buildings. I left Tammy by a massive chestnut that seemed to absorb her into its shadows. Then I climbed a five-bar gate and followed a hawthorn hedge that went far beyond the farm buildings. At the end of the hedge I turned left into a field of barley and the sloping ground led down to the farm. The farmhouse itself was a long low structure of Kentish clapboard and tiles. The moonlight made diamond patterns on the leaded windows so that the house looked like a film set, empty and abandoned. I saw the headlights of a solitary car passing up the lane below the house. There was no movement at any of the windows but I stood waiting for another ten minutes. As I waited I felt uneasy. The whole thing seemed ridiculous. I could be on the boat, snug and comfortable on Birdham Pool, or in the bay at Santa Margherita. What the hell was a man of fifty doing standing in damp grass in the middle of the night waiting his chance to break into a country house? All because a man I'd only met a couple of times seemed to be missing. I looked at my watch and it was time to start.

On the way down the garden hedge I scared a rabbit and he scared me. All the windows were tightly closed. The french windows would have come open with a knife but it would have left marks on the frames. The back door had a safety-lock and it took nearly three minutes to get it open. It gave on to a large farm-style kitchen. Mavis Trevor hadn't washed up for a couple of days. Horsey women get like that. There was a hall with a brick fireplace and then a large living room dominated by a big wide inglenook with a massive bressummer beam. Beneath the main back window was an old-fashioned desk and that was my target for tonight.

In the two front drawers were heaps of untidy stationery, ledgers, visiting cards and maps. In the three left-hand drawers were rosettes won at horse shows, pedigree forms, and bills and receipts for horse sales and food. The two bottom drawers on the right-hand side were locked. They came open with a knife and a wire paperclip. There was a large thick manilla envelope at the top of the middle drawer. I slid out the contents. They were photographs. Photographs of Mavis Trevor and Daphne Lakeman-Hart. 10 x 8 black and white glossies, unretouched and sharp as a razor. Mavis Trevor looked huge and around her pelvis she wore a harness that supported a crude phallus. In the pictures where she was coupling with Daffers it was reminiscent of King Kong and Fay Wray. But what made them so obscene was not the pathetic action but the look on the two faces. The girl's eyes were closed in a painful ecstasy and the woman's face contorted in brutal domination. I suppose some men must look like that, but God help the women who suffer them. I took a couple for the archives and slid the others back. There were two more envelopes of photographs. The thin one contained photographs of horses. Stallions riding mares, their long necks stretched and arched. White teeth gripping manes and wild, wicked eyes. Compared with the women they were beautiful. The third envelope was packed tight with photographs of different sizes. Some glossy, some matt. There were aerial views of stately homes and industrial complexes. Streets of shops and architectural details. When I broke in, I wasn't sure what I was after but I knew I wanted that packet. In the bottom drawer were piles of newspaper cuttings. Classified advertisements for second-hand cars, job vacancies, household goods and horses for sale. Some were old enough to have yellowed. I locked the drawers, picked up the envelope and went back to the kitchen. I walked back along the garden hedge and then down the field to the lane. Tammy was shivering at the big tree. It was 4 a.m. as we went over Battersea Bridge, and an hour later we were in bed.

I phoned Mario just after ten. There was a nice catamaran for sale at La Spezia. I said no. There was a fifty-foot Akerboom going at Genova and a sixty-five-foot De Vries for sale at Rapallo. I told him to take options on both for ten days. He didn't seem keen. He didn't actually refuse but he came very near it and when I started quizzing him he changed the subject. There were a dozen or so letters. Everything was fine. A vague air of why didn't I leave it all to him instead of worrying my pretty head. Mafalda was fine and so was he. When I hung up I felt uneasy. No reason why, except the training in 1940 and thirty years' experience in side-stepping nasty things heading my way.

When I asked the duty officer for Superintendent Haynes I remembered that he was on holiday. I hung up before they came back with the news. I took a taxi to the *News of the World* building and after some lies and chit-chat I was loosed down to their back-numbers section. I looked through 260 issues and made a long list and a few notes.

Back at the Hilton I picked up Tammy and had them bring up the hired car from the underground garage. I drove around London and the suburbs for six hours till I was sure of what I wanted.

Back at the Hilton I ordered our meal and we bathed while we were waiting. After we had eaten, we went through into Tammy's room. For over an hour I played jigsaw puzzles on the floor with the photographs from the big envelope. On my *News of the World* list I crossed off twelve items out of the twenty. The phone rang at ten. There was a person-to-person call for me from Nice. The operator at the French end checked twice that I was Monsieur Max Farne and she spelt my name out carefully in the international code – Foxtrot-Alfa-Romeo-November-Echo. There was the usual clunking and clicking as she made the connection and then I heard Mario's voice. It sounded urgent and concerned.

'Is that you, Max?'

'It's me all right, Mario. What's wrong?'

'Don't come back, Max.'

'Why on earth not?'

'There would be trouble.'

'What d'you mean – the police?'

'Look, Max, I cannot tell you. I came out of Italy to speak to you. Don't come back, Max; I'll settle everything for you here and transfer the money to you.'

'Tell me what's wrong then, Mario.'

I heard him sigh. 'Max, there are people – people of influence who would harm you.'

'You mean the police?'

'They could perhaps be used – but no, not the police.'

'What kind of people, Mario?'

'I cannot say more. It would be dangerous. Let's just say people of politics.'

'Mario, that's crazy. I don't have any interest in politics – not even English politics.'

'Max, I cannot say more. I say only do not come back, it will be dangerous. To say more would be dangerous for me. Please do as I say, Max.' And he hung up.

I found it difficult to imagine Mario frightened. I sat down in an armchair and Tammy came in from her room.

'Who was it?'

'A guy on the French Riviera wants a Hatteras boat.'

'What are all the photographs about, Max?'

I looked at her as she sat in the other chair. It wasn't fair to drag her into this, whatever 'this' turned out to be. I had thought I was beginning to make sense but Mario's call made my vague theory ridiculous. I stood up and poured us a drink. As I handed Tammy her glass I said, 'You know, young Tammy, I don't know anything about you except that you're beautiful.'

She smiled slightly, head on one side and looked at me as she sipped.

'What d'you want to know, Max?'

'Tell me about your family.'

'My father died when I was four. Broke his neck hunting. My second stepfather is a stockbroker. My mother's a bitch but she likes the life he gives her so she'll never leave him. He hates my guts, thinks I'm a chip off the old block, both old blocks. Thinks Daddy was a phoney and feckless.' She watched for my reaction.

'What *was* he like?'

'Everyone says he was a charmer. Handsome, gay – but he *was* feckless. Mother was in a mess when he died. No money and me and my sister to bring up. Now she's found it pays to keep the peace and we don't see one another.'

'And what about you?'

She shrugged. 'Drop-out, mixed-up, feckless, a hanger-on.'

'Serious boyfriends?'

She shook her head. 'Lots of lovers – no friends.'

'Why?'

She pursed her soft lips and looked up and across at me, one eye closed.

'They like my pretty face and my boobs. They never notice anything else. When they get used to those, it's over.' She laughed, but not with her eyes. 'You'd be surprised, Max, how soon they tire of what they once pleaded for. Short as a week and never longer than a few months.'

'And you?'

'I don't care any more, Max. It doesn't please me when they want me. I don't grieve any more when it's over.'

'Any more?'

She put her hands through her thick hair and pushed it behind her ears and her shoulders. Her head went back as if sorting out her thoughts visually on the ceiling. Her throat had a beauty all its own.

'In the beginning I was stupid. I mistook their lust for love. Thought somebody might care about me.' Her head came down and she smiled. 'Usual girl stuff. Not to worry.'

'Can I ask you some more about Dixon?'

'Sure.'

'What was his relationship with Mavis Trevor?'

'That was very odd. She was around quite a lot. She behaved like a partner. She'd got money in the company of course but my impression sometimes was that she told him what to do. Gave him orders. I came in sometimes when they had been talking and she'd start to leave and then sort of tell him not to forget what had been agreed. He went down to her place about once a month and generally came back the same day. She talked a lot on the phone to Daphne.'

'Did you ever go down to Penshurst with him?'

'God, no. I didn't even know where the place was until you took me. Just the name of it, that's all.'

'Did Daphne ever go?'

'Yes. She generally went with him. To take notes and all that.'

'Notes of what?'

'I don't really know. I had an impression of meetings of some sort.'

'And what was he like with the rich bitch?'

She laughed. 'Oh, that was very different. She wanted

to marry him. There was no business stuff there. She put up most of the bread when he started so he had to keep her happy.'

'And the childhood sweetheart?'

'Never saw her. He talked about her as if she was something special. I don't really think she was, he just had her in the background to keep the rest of us at bay.'

I decided not to tell her about Mario's warning. What she had told me didn't alter what I had been thinking. It was like a big white jigsaw with no picture and no straight bits.

Half-asleep I reached for my watch on the bedside table. It was nearly ten. Tammy was still sleeping, her rounded arms together and outstretched with her hands tucked under the pillow. I slid out of the bed and used the phone in Tammy's room to get us breakfast.

The photographs and the lists were still lying on the floor, the corners beginning to curl in the dry air of the central heating. I took the double tray from the waiter and set it beside our bed. I stroked the smooth shoulder gently to waken her and in a few moments she stirred and rolled over. She smiled as she saw the fresh orange juice in my hand. She drank it slowly as she eased her way back into the world. She was a great breakfast girl and the cornflakes and bacon and eggs went down with gusto. She leaned back on the pillows and in unlady-like fashion, licked her lips as she smiled at me with her soft peachy mouth. I'd have liked to have been the man who cared about her without having her, but it wasn't on, it was too late. I'd have to settle for caring and having. The pink tips of her big, inviting breasts had hardened and she smiled as she saw me looking. My hands closed over the firm mounds as she held out her arms. Like all the rest I couldn't wait to get in her.

It was midday by the time it was over and we'd showered. I was dressed and Tammy was curled up in the armchair reading one of the morning papers. She was reading my horoscope aloud, '... and today is a day for Scorpios to cement relationships. With the entry of Venus money matters will be disturbed. Avoid making any financial decision today.' She laughed and looked up at me. 'We'd better both go back to bed and do some cementing, Max.' She seemed more sure of herself. Maybe I was doing some good.

'Temperatures in London in the low seventies ... the first Test match starts today ... a lady in a divorce case says husband wanted to be with her all the time ... Judge says this behaviour abnormal and grants lady decree nisi ... four ex-wives disputing millionaire's will ... left all his bread to a stripper and the MCC ... girl shot in West End offices, the police are ... My God, Max, my God, look at this.'

She was white-faced and her hands trembled as she held up the paper.

It was only a couple of paragraphs.

BLONDE SECRETARY SHOT

Police are investigating the death of Miss Daphne Lakeman-Hart. An office cleaner discovered the body at 8 p.m. in the West End offices where she was employed, and informed the police. We understand that Miss Lakeman-Hart had received several gunshot wounds.

Inspector Sainsbury, who is in charge of the
investigation, said that the police are treating the
case as one of murder. The cleaner, Mrs Joan Fox,
is being treated at St Thomas's Hospital for shock.

I phoned down for the midday editions of the *Evening
News* and the *Standard*. They added very little except
a picture of the girl and a further statement from Scotland
Yard that she had been shot five times, and that the
investigation was proceeding.

There was no mention of the murder on the BBC
news at one o'clock. The evening editions of the papers
had cut it to a single paragraph.

When I read about the five shots, I knew I ought to
have guessed that it would happen. Either that, or she
would have disappeared. I was worried about Tammy
now. I phoned the Penshurst number and, when Mavis
Trevor's voice replied, I hung up.

'Tammy, I'll be out for about four hours. I want you
to stay here and don't answer the door to anyone. If
the phone rings, lift the receiver and listen. If nobody
speaks, hang up. When I come back I'll phone from
the lobby so you'll know it's me.'

They had brought the car up for me from the underground park and it was waiting at the back of the hotel
by the flower shop. I goosed her hard all the way to
Penshurst and then drove slowly up the lane. I parked
the car well short of the big house and walked to the
entrance to the stables. There was a small gate set in
the privet hedge between the house and the farm buildings and I walked carefully up the small concrete path

68

along the side of the house. There were deckchairs on the lawn and the french windows were both open. Although it was still light outside I could see lights on in the big living room. I walked past the kitchen door and looked into the living room. Mavis Trevor was on the phone. As I stepped inside she was just hanging up. As she bent to read a paper beside the phone I coughed and said, 'Good evening, Miss Trevor.'

She turned violently with half fright, half anger. Her face was flushed and the thick grey hair stood out from her head. Her mouth showed her unattractive teeth and her jaw was set with aggression.

'What the hell are you doing here? Get out. Get out, I say, or I'll call the police.'

I held up a hand to calm her down and I saw her eyes flicker over the room looking for a weapon.

'I don't mind if you call the police, Mavis. You go right ahead.'

She reached tentatively for the phone and then changed her mind. Her hand patted the springy Friar Tuck hair and did nothing for it, but it was an oddly feminine gesture which showed that she was working on old reflexes. Then she drew a deep breath.

'What is it you want, Mr Farne?'

'I want your help, Mavis.'

That gave her back her aggression and she stood hands on hips. The archetypical butch.

'I can't help you in any way, Mr Farne, so just . . .'

'Mavis, you'd better sit down as it's going to take some time.'

With little gestures of protest she sat. And I sat too. I looked across at her and sorted out the words.

'Why did you kill the girl?'

Her hand went to her mouth in shock. It wasn't the question she'd expected. She seemed paralysed and I waited. Then she was trembling and the trembling turned to shaking. She shook as if in the throes of an ague. She tried to speak and her lower jaw shook so violently that no words would form. Her arms were spread to steady her shaking body as the spasms took over. It lasted for almost five minutes and all the time her bloodshot eyes stared at my face. Then it was over, suddenly and completely, and her eyes closed as her head fell back and she sprawled in the chair, the thick woollen stockings twisted and sagging on her sturdy legs. The tears poured down her face but she made no noise. I couldn't afford to be merciful. I needed to know a lot more. It was obvious that in talking to me at all the girl had been suspect. When it went further than talking, they had decided she was too dangerous. That I'd guessed. But the five shots were not true to the pattern. Professional killers who need to fire two shots are on the way out. Five shots are the mark of crimes of passion and Mavis Trevor had seen the girl and me on the big leather couch. That was what I surmised before I came down. But I wanted to know who 'they' were. I had some clues but they only indicated the general area of who was involved. I wanted some names. Just one name would do.

When I moved towards Mavis Trevor, her wet eyes opened and her mouth sagged.

'Miss Trevor, I'll get you a doctor.'

Her voice quavered. 'No, no. Don't do that.' And she tried to shake her head.

'Do you know where Pat Dixon is?'

Her head shook and there was saliva on her lips. 'No . . . don't know . . . I swear,' and I believed her.

'Is he dead?'

The protuberant eyes looked away and her left hand started shaking again. There wasn't much time left.

'Pat Dixon was part of the gang, wasn't he?'

She nodded slowly and the words came out thickly. 'Just . . . just keeping it . . . sending it . . . away.'

Her head fell forward and I lifted it gently and held it.

'Who were the others?'

Her breathing was heavy and she groaned with each breath. 'I'm afraid . . .' and she cried as she tried to turn her face away.

'Who's D.T., Mavis?'

But no words would come. Her eyes looked up pathetically at mine.

'Is he the boss?'

She nodded slightly and closed her eyes with fear at even that gesture.

'Give me a name, Mavis . . . just one name. Then no more questions. I'll get you help and they'll soon get you well again.'

I held my hand under her jaw and I could smell the bile in her mouth. I moved my hands so that they cradled her face. Her head was so heavy I had to spread my fingers to take the load.

'The name, Mavis . . . just one of them.'

Her head shook with the effort but the words were audible. 'Price . . . Arthur Price,' and the hot vomit surged over my arm.

71

I cleaned up. Phoned the doctor and was off. I stood in the shadow of Tammy's big tree and waited till I saw the old Mini turn and park. The doctor reached for his bag, slammed the car door and hurried up the path to the house. There was a band of light from the open front door.

It seemed a long drive back to London and it seemed unbelievable that it was past midnight. I was exhausted but I knew I was on the way to finding out what had happened to Dixon. Arthur Price was a name that I'd seen several times in the basement library of the *News of the World*. Arthur Price had nearly won the Senior TT in 1950. It was 'nearly' because he took one of the humpbacks too fast and parted from his machine. He had been unconscious for three weeks and when he had recovered he was told that his reflexes would never be sharp enough for the Isle of Man again. Arthur Price had opened a small garage in Wandsworth. The first conviction had been for converting stolen cars, and the second was for 'taking a motor vehicle or other conveyance without authority'. They had failed on a 'conspiracy to rob' charge. Arthur Price was a freelance 'transport consultant' to most of the *ad hoc* gangs put together for major robberies. But after the first two convictions Arthur Price had learned a thing or two and he'd had the advice and protection of a sharp criminal solicitor. With Arthur Price on the payroll, getting there and getting away were planned to a second. It made a difference in recruiting specialists if you could say Arthur was already on board.

I phoned Tammy from the lobby and she answered straight away. The flower shop was long closed.

Everything was closed, so I gave the porter a couple of quid and we went around the restaurant nicking the flowers from the tables. We made up a nice unwieldy bunch.

I tapped on the door and Tammy let me in, big-eyed as I offered my Harvest Festival. I don't think anyone had ever given her a bunch of flowers before. While she arranged the flowers in a couple of vases, I sat with a whisky and told her the night's saga.

'I don't see why the five shots made you think of Mavis Trevor.'

'I guess it was those photographs. Two slugs will finish anybody. People who use five have to hate a lot . . . or love a lot.'

Six

There was the usual jam on Putney Bridge. The river looked like thick brown chocolate laced with bottles, cans, driftwood and dead cats. Only a hundred years ago the apprentice boys were rioting because they were forced to eat so much fresh salmon from the Thames. The mass of cars shuffled forward fifty yards and I sat for another ten minutes while a traffic cop sorted us out, and then went on to Upper Richmond Road and turned left. A mile further on and I turned into the maze of small roads on the edge of Wandsworth.

The TT garage had only a single petrol pump. There was a longish brick building front with no windows but a big sliding door that would take two cars. It was closed. There were two big, high, swing doors that gave on to a yard. The yard itself was covered with those hard blue Victorian bricks. Everywhere was swept and clean. There was a small door let into a big slider and it was already open. The workshops were lit with strip lights and there were long peg-board panels on the walls with dozens of tools clipped on them. A man was spraying a car in a spray booth down the far end and there must have been twenty cars in the place.

There was a small glass-fronted office to the left and I knocked and went in. A podgy young girl sat at an old typewriter and a man with a pencil behind his ear was looking at a small pile of papers. He was broad but not tall and built like a solid barrel. His shirt left a four-inch gap down to his belt where it couldn't make it across his chest and belly, his fly was unzipped to give him breathing space. The girl looked at me and then at fatty, who ignored me while he sorted out problems of State. He looked ex-army to me, vintage World War Two. Some dark brown hair still left was plastered smoothly to his bullet head. The last surviving Brylcreem boy. His shirt was khaki, but not the khaki of any army I knew. A nasty yellow sort of khaki. Finally he condescended to look up. The little piggy eyes were ready for a quarrel if that was possible. When he had looked me over he didn't speak, just jerked his head in interrogation. There must still be little old ladies around who respond to that sort of thing. I said nothing but I looked a lot and finally he leaned one thick arm on the counter, sucked a tooth speculatively, and then said, 'Yeah?'

'Is Arthur Price around?'

He put one thick finger in his ear and raked around, examined his nail and wiped his finger on the filthy trousers.

'Wha' d'ya want wiv Arfer?'

'Mind your own business, chum. Just tell me where he is.'

The little girl kept her head down and pecked slowly

at an invoice, and fatty adjusted his dentures with his top lip. Then he shook his head and turned back to the paperwork. Without looking up he said, 'E's out.'

In the workshop there was a man bending over an XJ6 and I walked over to him. I heard fatty coming up behind me. I asked the man where Arthur Price might be and before he could answer the fat man pulled at my shoulder.

'I've told you, mate. 'E's out. Now sod off, you're trespassin'.' It wasn't often he invoked the law and he rather liked it. I turned to look at the red smirking face.

'You've got a notice outside saying you do car repairs. You're open. That notice is an invitation to enter. That means there's no trespass. But you . . . fat boy, could be causing a breach of the peace.'

The pig eyes closed even further and the thick right arm came round like a falling tree. I ducked and helped it on its way and hooked my foot in his instep. His left foot made a lovely fulcrum and it would have made a good diagram in a book on dynamics, illustrating the effect of weight times velocity around a fixed point. It was like scaffolding collapsing on a building as his legs crossed and buckled, and he fought for balance. The thick arm flailed and snatched for support and didn't find any. His head was diverted a little on the way down by the curve on the Jag's front bumper. He struggled to get up and I bridged my foot from his hand to his wrist and he lay back wondering what had happened. I looked down at him. His kind would have one more half-hearted go, get clouted, and call it a day. But fat boy had had enough and, when I turned to the mechanic, fat boy stayed still.

'Is Arthur Price around?'

'He's in the Ivy, across the road.'

The pub was almost empty and the landlord pointed out Price at a table in the far corner. I walked over and Arthur Price looked at me with raised eyebrows but an air of amiability. He signalled with a fork for me to sit down.

He looked remarkably like me. Just over six foot. A tanned, leathery face. Big shoulders and large working hands. He went on eating his lamb chop and peas. Not rudely, just a man with things to do.

'Mr Price?'

''Smee, fella. What can I do for ya?'

'Can I get you a drink?'

The blue eyes looked at me as he shook his head.

'Don't drink, fella. What is it, a re-spray?'

I leaned back to watch his face.

'No. It's about Pat Dixon.'

He didn't look up and he didn't stop eating. His knife was scooping gravy on to the potatoes.

'Oh 'ar. And who's he?'

'He was in the rag-trade, Mr Price, and he looked after stolen money and goods till the heat was off. Sent it overseas for people. And he's dead.'

His head jerked up at that and the bright blue eyes were very alert.

'Who says he's dead?'

'You know him then?'

He waved his knife dismissively. I noticed how muscled the brown arms were. His mouth looked hard and his eyes looked angry. He spoke slowly, saying each word separately.

'Who says he's dead?'

He chewed some food and swallowed it carefully. His head was to one side looking out of the window. Then he looked back at me, stood up, and said quietly, 'You'd better come back to the office with me.'

He nodded to the barman and we walked out into the sunshine and crossed the road to the garage.

Just inside the garage's big gates he stopped suddenly, and then turning, he called to a man in the workshop.

'Joe, turn that broom the other way up. It's getting spoiled.' The man walked over to the far wall and turned a broom so that its bristles were at the top. Price stood and waited, watching while it was done. Then we moved on. 'Waste not, want not, I always say.' I was struck by the cool detachment of a man who was going to talk about a murder in a few seconds, caring about the cost of a yard broom.

In the office he told the girl to go and get her meal. There was no sign of fat boy. Price lifted a decrepit internal phone and pressed a button.

'Joe, have you seen Mike?'

He listened intently and then slowly looked up at me. I got the impression that Mike and fat boy were one, and Price was getting the saga of our encounter. He nodded from time to time and then said, 'OK,' and hung up slowly.

'I gather you've already met my foreman.'

'The fat fellow?'

He nodded and leaned back, pointing at a chair.

'Have a seat.'

As I made myself comfortable he held a long jack-knife with both hands and was concentrating on cutting a deep nick in the table edge. We all have some device to help sort out our thoughts and this was obviously his. After a few moments of silence he laid down the knife and screwed up his eyes as he looked at me.

'Tell me about Dixon. Why do you think he's dead?'

I told him about the letter and the boat, and a few more details. Without him saying a word he'd confirmed everything I'd suspected, and he was so sure of himself that he didn't bother to confirm or deny what wasn't worth discussing. After a few minutes' thought he reached for the dusty phone and dialled a number.

'Is Harry there? This is Arthur Price, missus.'

He got the knife to work again and then put it down and leaned forward.

'Harry, where's Dixon?'

He listened carefully and nodded a couple of times.

'Thanks, Harry. I've sold the Capri by the way.'

He looked at me again. 'What's your name, fella?'

'Farne. Max Farne.'

'Not a copper?'

'No.'

'Thought not. Dixon's done a bolt. They know he had a booking by air for Milan. About the time of that letter. That's all they know. Now what about you?'

'What about me?'

He smoothed his hand on his jaw. Deciding something.

'I reckon you know too much, fella.'

'About what?'

He looked up from his table-cutting and smiled.

'You're a cheeky bugger. Coming into the Ivy. Asking about Dixon, bold as brass. Where'd you live?'

'I'm staying at the Hilton but I live on a boat so I've no fixed address.'

He liked the 'no fixed address' bit, especially when it was coupled with the Hilton.

'Why d'you want Dixon?'

'I want to sort out the boat business.'

He nodded approvingly.

'You've not made any contact with the others, have you?'

'No. Just you.'

A big hand came across the table. I shook it and thanked him for his help and went back to the car.

I rather liked Arthur Price and I could easily see that his attention to detail and his self-confidence would lift the morale of a bunch of rogues. There was something he'd said that rang a bell but I couldn't place it. It would come.

I phoned Mavis Trevor's number but there was no reply. I phoned the doctor. Miss Trevor was in the Intensive Care Unit at Pembury Hospital. I phoned the hospital. She was on the danger list with no visitors allowed. She had suffered a severe coronary thrombosis and her condition was grave.

'Tammy, let's go and get you some more clothes.'

'Great. But why?'

'We're off back to Italy again.'

'You going to forget Pat Dixon?'

'Put him in store for a bit, honey, that's all. By the way, how did you get yourself out to Italy?'

'Pat got me a ticket to Milan and some bread.'

'Air ticket?'

'Yes. A return.'

'You still got the return bit?'

She shuffled around in the old duffle bag and came up with a crumpled airline ticket booklet. It was booked at the Kensington and Hampstead Travel Bureau. I found them down Adam and Eve Mews off Kensington High Street. They booked our seats to Milan and then I asked them about Tammy's booking. They traced that and we moved on to Pat Dixon. They found the booking. Yes, the outward flight had been used and better still they'd booked his hotel. It was a little place at the back of the via Marconi, the Hotel Napoleone.

Tammy and I spent an hour at Jaeger's and even longer at the Café Royal. She was wearing one of the new dresses, white silk with a pleated skirt. The waiter made a fuss of her and she looked beautiful, young, and relaxed. I booked us on to the train to Milan via Zurich. I was certain that I would be contacted in Milan and I wanted it to be on my own ground in my own good time.

It was first light as we left the St Gotthard Pass, and I woke Tammy to see the orchards and hillsides as the mist rolled over them so that all was in the soft focus of early summer. People astir on small country stations stood back as the train swept past and waved as they saw our uncovered window. It was just after six when we arrived at Milan and I lodged our cases at the left luggage office. All Italy was in the station precinct; the pin-stripe suits and fur and tweeds from our train and then from the far side the travel-weary Sicilians and Calabrians from the '*mezzogiorno*' in their ill-fitting

slept-in suits, all come to make a living in Milan where
the standard morning greeting was *'buon lavoro'*, 'good
work' not just 'good day'. Small cherubim waited with
pale madonnas for unshaven Josephs. I loved them all.
Early morning typists and secretaries walked long-
legged from their hips while their tight skirts played
noughts and crosses with their saucy rumps.

Out in the street the sun was already slanting its
westward shadows and it felt like being a Sforza
checking the estates as we walked down the via
Marconi. We had coffee with fresh rolls, butter and
honey. I bought two *gettone* from the waiter and went
over to the wall-phone and dialled. The last time I
had dialled that number was in 1943. It was the night
of July 9 and I told them that our lot would be landing
in Sicily the next day. Two days later I was there
when the OVRA raided the house. They didn't find
either of us but they took away the signora and when
she came back six weeks later she had to walk with
sticks until the bones in her feet had come together
again.

'*C'e la signora?*'

'*Si. Aspett' un momento.*'

'Signora Mondadori. *Chi parla?*'

'*Vorrei affittare un appartamenta per due mesi, ne
ha da affirmi?*'

'*Certo, ma chi parla per favore?*'

'Capitano Farne.'

There was a moment's silence and then came the
flood. We walked round there with Tammy's bags.
There were still tears on the signora's cheeks as she
hugged me tightly and put her head on my shoulder.

Then she was '*la signora*' again. Letting cats out of bags all over the place.

'And the pretty *bambina*. Always they pretty when he bring them here. Always too young. Come on, let me show you where I can give you.'

She sat on the bed while we unpacked and we talked of long ago days and long ago people. It must have sounded like the Crusades to Tammy. She turned to the girl. 'When he come he *tenente*, next time *capitano*, and after Anzio he come *maggiore*. English impossible, they think it all a game.' The intense brown eyes looked at Tammy. 'He sometimes come here just to play chess with me when my son killed. Ver' good man to us all times. Make a good 'usband. Yes?' Tammy smiled and looked at me with a knowing look.

When she left us Tammy said, 'Have you been back here since the war?'

'Only twice. The last time was ten or eleven years ago.'

'It's like the long-lost son coming home.'

'She's a good woman, a brave woman too.'

Tammy sat on the bed beside me with her hand on my knee. They were gentle trusting fingers and they ought to have had at least one ring on them by now. I thought I'd better get around to business.

'We'll stay here tonight, Tammy, and tomorrow I'll go and book in at the hotel on my own. If anyone is expecting me, they'll expect me today. I've got a hunch they'll make contact but I don't want it to be too easy. I'll contact you by phone, sweetie. Let you know what's going on.'

'That's why you booked us on the plane but we came on the train?'

'That's it.'

'Can't I know more?'

'You remember all the photographs at the hotel. They were the places they planned to rob. Mavis Trevor was their contact with Pat Dixon. Right from the start of his business they used him. After a big raid they needed to get rid of the stuff quickly. That was Dixon's job. I think it went down to the farm. Then when the heat was off, say after six months, Dixon would switch it out of the country for them. The rag-trade was ideal; he'd got overseas customers everywhere. Little Daffers probably knew what was going on and they probably thought she'd talked too much to me. Whoever Dixon worked for didn't kill him; they don't know what's happened to him. I'm sure of that. I don't know why he bolted or why he's been knocked off, but I'll find out.'

'Why here?'

'The chap at Santa Margherita who came visiting with the gun expected to find Dixon on the boat. He was sent by the London end. That phone call from France last week was from Mario. He said there'd be trouble if I went back to Santa Margherita. Didn't say who would provide the trouble but he went to the trouble of going to Nice to phone me. He wouldn't do that if he wasn't really worried. Mario doesn't scare easily.'

'Is it because of the man with the gun?'

'I don't know, honey. That's probably part of it but Mario said the pressure wasn't directly from the police. I really don't know.'

'Why do you bother at all, Max?'

'Partly bloody-mindedness. Nobody's going to do anything about Dixon. There's nothing to go on and there's nobody with any right to pressure the police. And which police anyway. If he *was* killed, where was it done? I don't really give a damn about the robberies, it's only money, but I can't stomach these bastards just calmly killing off people as if they were animals to be slaughtered. I've got a slight vested interest. Nearly twelve thousand quid in fact. Dixon paid for the Fjord. It's still mine in law. If he's dead, I don't intend handing it over to Arthur Price and his mates as part of the estate.'

Tammy looked up at me frowning.

'You're a funny mixture, Max. Kind, gentle and all that, but kind of savage inside.'

'I'm sure you're right, kid, but let's not dwell on it.'

I stood up and went over to the small window. I called her over. Down in the narrow street was a knife-grinder with his wood-frame cycle. His two fingers lightly touched the knife blades and a shower of orange and white sparks curved over the heads of the children who were watching. They were all clean, well-dressed and happy, but the people who lived in this street were grindingly poor. You don't need a Society for the Prevention of Cruelty to Children in Italy. Cats and dogs have to be quick on their feet but not children. And girls don't end up like Tammy in Italy either. Their hearts may get broken but not their spirits. Only in England's green and pleasant land do social workers and psychiatrists have to keep finding new excuses for babies in dustbins.

Mama Mondadori got us a splendid lunch of minestrone and stufato, spiced beef cooked in white wine with tomatoes, carrots and celery. After lunch we went down to the Parco Sempione and sat by the big lake and watched the children playing. In one of the side streets near the Stazione Nord was an old cinema. My partisan group used it as a dead letter drop, and in those days you sat for ten minutes watching the film and then headed for the crummy toilets and dabbled in the cistern for messages stuffed in Hatu packs. War or no war, we saw a lot of Bette Davis and Barbara Stanwyck. It took time to find it again, it seemed to have shrunk or something, but it was showing *Via col Vento* and we sat through the short version that lasts only three hours. The story of Scarlet O'Hara and Rhet Butler still seemed good stuff but just to relieve the tension they stuffed in a cartoon and a newsreel about halfway through. We saw Signor Fanfani opening something, a pile-up the previous week on the Autostrade del Sol, the Pope receiving a delegation about the divorce law, and a pack of politicians hollering about how they would make all us voters into millionaires. There was a nice trailer of *Bianca Neve a le sette nani* for my companion, who admitted to being able to identify by name all the seven dwarfs. The sound was overwhelming and, when we came out into the street, we closed our eyes against the white hot sun but the city noises sounded like gentle music to our battered ears.

In the evening I took Mama Mondadori with us to her favourite restaurant on the Piazza del Duomo, and we ate slowly while Mama rocked in agony at the comedian's jokes about the human condition, the Pope and politicians in general. Tammy and I danced a couple of shaky tangos and I sent a note to the orchestra that cost me drinks all round, but they played me the lovely waltz the Italians call the 'Waltz of the Candles', *'Valzer delle Candele'*. And we call it 'Auld Lang Syne'. There were knowing smiles from the band as I waltzed my pretty blonde, and men with grey hair, or no hair, waltzed with their companions. And some of us were thinking to ourselves of other girls in other days, when Germans sat at the same tables and the band had played, and for no sane reason we'd got a kick out of dancing to the gentle, alien tune that the Germans never recognized.

It was past midnight when we got back to our room. It was large and clean with a low, friendly ceiling. The walls were plain white paint and there were no pictures. The furniture was old, simple, wooden stuff from Tuscany, hand-carved with simple chisel marks and here and there an adventurous rosette where an artisan boy had tried his 'prentice hand with a gouge.

Tammy was on the bed, her back curved as she leaned forward, her long arms stretched past her knees to touch her feet. Her head rested on her knees and turned to watch me with the thick blonde hair about her shoulders. She watched me as I carried out the male equivalent of putting in curlers. Laid out carefully on the latest edition of *Oggi* were the bits and pieces of a model 1934 Beretta pistol. They were, as the army used to say, clean bright and slightly oiled. There is a much later model, the 1951, with another 200 feet per second muzzle velocity. It takes an extra round and has some nice points. But it weighs nearly three quarters of a pound more, and that can make

even bigger holes in pocket linings than its prede-
cessor. And the later model has a button type safety-
catch that needs a second hand when I use it. I hadn't
been able to lay hands on any 9 mm. Corto since the
war so I used good old .380 ACP. I loaded seven
rounds into the box magazine and rammed it up with
the heel of my hand. I loaded two spare magazines
and stuffed them in the chamois leather flaps in my
jacket. I turned the safety-catch away from me and
I was all ready for beddy-byes.

Tammy had one eye screwed up as she surveyed the
scene.

'It's kind of romantic, really.'

'What . . . the pistol?'

'No, being with you in Milan. That you know it so
well. That you were here all those years ago. And did
things.'

'Like Old Tyme dancing on BBC radio, you mean?'

'Yes, sort of nostalgic.'

'Even nostalgia ain't what it used to be, sweetie.'

And I slid my hand to that peachy rump where it
curved into the white sheets. And while I stroked her
she said, 'Tell me the words of that song, Max. The
waltz.'

'In Italian?'

'Yes.'

'*Domani tu mi lascerai e piu non tornerai, domani . . .*'

'What is it in English?'

'Tomorrow I shall leave you and then I'll never return,
tomorrow . . .'

She cried out, 'No more. I don't like it.'

She put her hand out and stroked my shoulder.

'You won't leave me and not come back. Will you, Max?'

'No, Tam. I'll be back but it may take a few days.'

'Do you really think they'll come?'

'They'll come all right, honey.'

Seven

The Hotel Napoleone is what the Michelin guide describes as '*un albergo di buon confort*'. The six steps up to the portico were of creamy marble, and in the foyer there were no hostages to modernity. Necchi, Olivetti and Farina might never have existed for the influence that they had wielded in this small corner of Milan. Except for the lift, and here Mr Otis and his boys had obviously made a good pitch, for it was the latest model, with flashing lights to please all boyish hearts.

I checked in and as soon as I gave my name I sensed the red lights winking. The clerk looked up too quickly, and then was too obliging. When it was all settled up and the girl had my bag and the big brass key, I sent off the first little message.

'By the way, what room did my friend Mr Dixon have when he stayed here?'

'Signor Dixon, sir? An Englishman?'

'That's it.'

'Now when was that, sir? For the racing at Monza, maybe?'

'No. About three weeks ago.'

He shuffled through the register and then traced an entry as if he was just learning to read.

'Oh, here we are, sir . . . Signor Pat Dixon . . . from London . . . room forty-nine . . . with bath . . . two beds . . . *pensione completa* . . . that's it, sir . . . room number forty-nine.'

And he slapped the ledger closed in case I hadn't taken the hint.

My room was on the fifth floor at the front of the building, looking out on the busy street. The girl who had carried my bag unlocked the bathroom door and showed me the radio and TV switches. She was about eighteen, roughly five five in her shoes, and she wore her black dress uniform as if it were designed by Simonetta. She had one of those *jolie-laide* faces that were quick to smile and, when I spoke, she laughed and nodded.

'*Voi siete una Toscana, si?*'

'*Si, signor, e lei?*'

'*Sono Inglese.*'

'*Ma ché, tuparla Italiana com' un Calabrese.*'

And we both laughed at what was at least a half-insult. She was delighted with the thousand lire and she grinned a friendly, cheeky grin as she closed the door.

I unpacked and did all those simple things with hairs and pins that let you know if your stuff's been gone through while you were out. Then I sat on the bed and felt lonely. I wondered how long they'd take. They had probably sat all day at the airport at di Linate yesterday, waiting and wondering what had happened.

I opened my wallet and looked again at the note I had found in Dodds' pocket but it gave me nothing new. There was the piece torn from the newspaper with the racing results and I wondered why my friend Monty had kept it. I looked down the lists of racehorses' names. There were some names that were Italian like Giulietta and Pampino but they didn't mean anything to me. I was folding it up again when I noticed the other side. It was crammed with those small classified ads that keep our journals' cash-flow just above the low-tide mark. These were for services. Lovely girl graduates would escort me through an exciting evening when I was next in town. A girl named Karen would like to give me a relaxing massage. And then a whole host of people would rent me a van with driver for my removal to my new home. There was a strong impression that the driver could drive well by moonlight. And then one of the ads came leaping up off the page; it said 'D.T. No load available. Explain personally. P.D.' It was just one and a half lines in the middle of all the half-inch columns. And I was sure in that moment that I knew why Dixon was dead. And I guessed that some local in Europe who covered the gang's interests would be my awaited guest. I was desperately wrong about that but I couldn't have guessed the truth. And if I had, I'd have gone straight back to the airport.

I hung around the hotel that day, eating in the restaurant. I went out once to phone Tammy from a nearby café. Nobody followed me and nobody seemed to be watching me. I locked my room door at ten and slept soundly until nine o'clock the next morning. I sat in my bathrobe eating my breakfast and read my complimentary copy of *La Stampa*.

During the day I made myself visible. There were three cafés within a hundred yards of the hotel and I gave them all some custom. I window-shopped and bought a book of Italian poetry. Despite the creativity and the language, there isn't much really good Italian poetry. The classical stuff is overblown, but the new boys are coming along and poems and cappuccini go well together. I had a feeling I was being watched but although I did the basic checks I didn't spot anyone at it. If you make yourself into the sacrificial goat, you probably wind up your awareness anyway. Your imagination too.

It happened on the second day. I'd sat reading the paper at the Trattoria del Orso. It was almost empty and the only other customers were an old man and a middle-aged woman. I bought a *gettone* and asked for the phone. They pointed to a passageway that seemed to lead to the kitchen. I'd put in the metal disc and the dialling tone came up and somebody wanted to come past. I thought it was a waiter and pressed myself to the wall obligingly and shoved my finger in to dial the first number when a voice said very quietly, '*Stai tranquillo, amico,*' and a gun pressed hard in my back. There was nothing to be done. There was no room to move. It would have been the proverbial shooting fish in a barrel. He couldn't have missed if he had tried. He patted me, found the gun and pocketed it. He still went on patting. He'd played these games before. Then there was a rustling noise like a plastic bag and a pungent smell like petrol, and before I could think there was a big pad of cotton wool over my nose and mouth. He pushed me hard against the wall and then I went down a long, long slope with a tunnel and there was a noise like a car door banging. It was a nuisance when I was trying to sleep. I came to in a swirling mist and the car door banged again. A stray hand pulled on my jacket and the world swung around as I was pulled upright. I was sitting on the back seat of a car and the man watching me was a thick-set thug with shoulders like Henry Cooper. He was short and his arms were massive. One giant hand gripped my jacket to hold me up and the other held an old but useful Luger. As the mists rolled back I could see that the car was in a cobbled courtyard and before I could take it all in he pulled me to the door. He looked at my eyes and judged me fit for service. He gave another heave and I was standing on my plasticine legs outside the car. He walked me around the yard a time or two and then up some stone steps into a large cool hallway. There were beautiful marble statues and busts and a wide marble staircase. There must have been twenty steps but it felt like a hundred. At the top was an open area with white doors relieved with a gilded pattern of oak leaves. The carpet was white so that the whole area seemed to be bathed in a cool illumination.

As we walked across the deep-piled carpet a servant stood at the big double doors and, as if I were some special guest, he bowed and opened one of the doors. The big room was magnificent. The walls were a cool pale green with large murals that looked like Annigonni's.

On one wall was a wide panorama of Rome and on another the great spread of Firenze. The furniture was seventeenth century, polished and perfect as if it had just been made. The big armchairs and a fifteen-foot settee were in soft yellow leather. On the right was a superb desk and in the centre was a big circular glass-topped table with tropical fish beneath it.

A man stood there. He was over six feet tall and slim with delicate hands and small feet in black brogue shoes. His suit was a pale blue lightweight mohair that made his deep tan look even darker. His white hair was cropped to a crewcut and his dark brown eyes were big and gentle, but his mouth was edged by the deep-cut lines that came from making decisions and giving orders. He stood like a soldier, erect and alert, and he must have been in his early sixties. He was used to being looked at and he stood there unembarrassed till he reckoned I'd had my ration. As he put his hands behind him and walked forward he looked even more commanding, a little like the Duke of Edinburgh. About six feet away from me he stopped and waved me to one of the leather armchairs.

'Mr Farne, I'm sorry this had to be so melodramatic but it was the easiest way. My name is Timonetti, by the way, Dino Timonetti. Do please sit down.' He looked over my shoulder and dismissed his goon with a brief nod. He spoke beautiful English with no trace of accent. Or, if there was an accent, it was faintly American, not Italian. The severe patrician face reminded me of pictures I'd seen of Somerset Maugham. He waited until I sat down and then adjusted the leg of his trousers like my father used to do. A little upward pull and then you bent your knees. There was a thin manilla file cover on the settee beside him and a diamond in his ring sparkled as he reached for it. He opened it and started reading from a foolscap page of typing. Little excerpts like Tammy reading my horoscope.

'Now let us see. It's Maximilian Sigmund Farne. Age fifty-three. Born in Paris. Mother German, father English. Whitgift School, Croydon. Army 1939–48. Last rank Major. Usual Intelligence Corps training, then seconded SOE for three years. Worked in French group in Lyons and then Paris. Liaison officer with partisans in area Milano, Torino, La Spezia. Awarded Croce di Guerra by first Italian provincial government. DSO and a second recommendation which was turned down. Married Joanna Mary Spencer at Chelsea registry office on 4 September 1939. Divorced 24 October 1946. Ex-wife now living in Austin, Texas. In business as boat broker and sales. Business address c/o The Chandlery, Birdham Pool, Chichester, Sussex. Account number 90750552 at Barclays Bank, East Street, Chichester. Current account overdrawn £19.70. Deposit account £2,471. Numbered accounts at Basler Bundesbank Zürich, State Bank Liechtenstein and Third Bahamian Bank, Nassau. Has been questioned by police on several accounts in London, Paris, Santa Margherita, Dallas and Amsterdam. No charges brought on any occasion.' He looked up at me. 'And responsible for murdering a fellow countryman named Dodds in Santa Margherita.'

I looked back at him but I didn't respond. I don't always answer when people ask me questions and I never answer when they just make statements and lift their eyebrows.

'Why did you do that, Mr Farne?'

'Ask the *polizia* in Santa Margherita.'

He looked at me coldly and folded up the file and put it on the seat beside him. It was only then that the penny dropped about his name. I'd been guessing in English of course.

'Now, what is it you want, Mr Farne? It is possible that I could help you.'

'I want to know what happened to Pat Dixon and who did it.'

'Why do you want to know?'

'He was a client of mine.'

He raised his fine eyebrows even higher.

'And do you follow the lives of all your clients so assiduously?'

'Only those who get murdered.'

Signor Timonetti leaned back. His hands were beside him on the settee and his fingers were doing the 3rd Brandenburg as he looked at me pensively. Like good fathers look at bad sons. Like referees used to look at Jackie Charlton. Then he made the big decision and leaned forward.

'Let us speak hypothetically for a moment, Mr Farne. Suppose that your client Mr Dixon had been involved in crime and suppose that it was because of that involvement that he came to some harm?'

The pale blue eyes were watching me carefully.

'Signor Timonetti, you went to the trouble of doing a very thorough check on me. I saw you on a news reel yesterday making a political speech. I'd like to know how you are involved.'

He shook his handsome head slowly and pursed his lips.

'Mr Farne, I ask you, I beg you, to go home and forget all this. You are beginning to get into very deep waters. Far beyond what you think. You are in danger . . . great danger.'

'Tell me what has happened to Dixon and I'll think about it.'

He sighed and stood up, picking up the manilla folder. He walked across to the magazine desk, put the folder in a drawer and locked it from a bunch of keys on a ring. He looked at his watch.

'I think we should eat, Mr Farne.'

He pressed a button on the wall and when the servant came in he gave orders for lunch to be served. He escorted me, with all the courtesy he would have shown to an honoured guest, to the big doors near the window.

The table was set with superb glass and silver. There were places for three and a maid was arranging an extra place. There were bottles and glasses on a long sideboard. A girl and a man were standing at the far end of the table talking. The man had his back to me and Timonetti took my arm and took me over to them. The girl was beautiful with large soft brown Italian eyes, a wide mouth with firm outlines to her lips, and a fine nose. As Timonetti spoke to her, she smiled so that the wide mouth showed her teeth and the dimples near her high Slav cheeks.

'Mr Farne, let me introduce you. La signorina Sylva Polezzi and Avvocato Franceschini.'

The girl's hand was smooth and her handshake was gentle. Avvocato Franceschini nodded his head. He was a big man, tall with heavy shoulders, and a face as tanned and leathery as my own. His hair was wiry and still black although he must have been in his sixties, but every part of him spelt out a dynamic. From the forward thrust of his head to the planting of his feet there was great power and energy. As he looked me over his face was noncommittal but aware. A man used to judging men for action.

Timonetti pointed out our seats and the girl was opposite me. She really was beautiful with a healthy, glossy tan that was almost too deep for a girl. The lunchtime conversation was in English, which they all spoke perfectly, and was of London and Paris and people rather than events. An observer could not possibly have guessed that I was a virtual prisoner rather than the guest of honour. My opinions were sought on graphic design, music and literature, and we spent a lot of time on the Italian boatyards and their latest developments. Very briefly, from time to time, I was conscious of being probed on what I knew of current Italian politics. There was an air of quiet satisfaction when I confessed that I didn't know the names of the current President or Prime Minister. We got on to the capital requirements of setting up my type of operation in, say, Santa Margherita and I knew that I was being offered a bone. A bone with quite a lot of meat on it. I avoided the leading questions but it was the girl who finally nailed me. As her long brown arm reached forward to give me a light she said, 'I think you like Italy, Mr Farne.'

I smiled. 'I think it's Italians I like, Miss Pelozzi. Most countries have their beauty. Many others have sun. But only Italy has Italians.'

She smiled and gave a little laughing bow, but it was Timonetti who chipped in.

100

'What do you like about us, Mr Farne?'

I leaned back and thought before I spoke.

'I like the way they wear their hearts on their sleeves. Their warm-heartedness. Their pleasure in just being alive. Their indifference to politicians and governments.'

Avvocato Franceschini was not amused.

'Their indifference keeps us permanently on the verge of bankruptcy, Mr Farne.'

I shook my head. 'No, Avvocato. That's caused by politicians making promises they can't keep. And an aristocracy that doesn't give a damn.'

Timonetti nodded vigorously. 'For a man not interested in politics, you hold strong views, Mr Farne.'

'Signor Timonetti, as somebody once said, Fascists, Communists, Socialists and Conservatives have never even made a hen-coop. It's people who make things.'

Timonetti sat back and looked at me carefully.

'And what are we going to do with you, Mr Farne?'

'I think you should apologize for your hoodlum's behaviour and we'll forget that it happened.'

I saw Franceschini shake his head. But he left the talking to Timonetti. He smiled and stood up.

'Would you entertain Signorina Pelozzi for a few moments?'

The two men left us and I stood up and walked to the window. There was a small courtyard below and an Alfa parked facing the closed gates. A small fountain stood in the centre of the yard and there was enough breeze to fan the water in one direction. A man stood by the gate keeping watch. I went back to the table and looked at the girl. Around her slender throat was a black

101

band of moiré silk and it was held in place by a shield-shaped flat gold clasp. There was something engraved on the gold.

'Do they do this sort of thing very often, Miss Pelozzi?' The gaze was steady, calm and friendly.

'They're very powerful men, Mr Farne. They have influence at all levels. They are being very gentle with you in the circumstances.'

'What circumstances?'

'Your interest in Mr Dixon is beginning to interfere with important things. Things that are nothing to do with him in any way.'

'What happened to Dixon? Is he dead?'

She tapped the ash from her cigarette into a heart-shaped ashtray before she answered and she looked at my face for a few moments, making up her mind.

'Yes, he's dead. He did something very, very stupid that would have had serious consequences in this country.' Her lovely brown eyes looked into mine. 'Please believe me. He tried to interfere in things that were not his concern.'

'Politics?'

'In a way, but what he did was not political.'

'What was it?'

I thought for a moment she was going to tell me but the two men came back into the room. Timonetti wasted no time, but he was still polite and formally charming.

'Ah, Mr Farne. I've made arrangements for you to go to a villa of mine for a few days.' He looked at the girl. 'We should like you to accompany Mr Farne, Sylva.'

We went south when we left Milan and at about twenty kilometres down the autostrada the goon pulled over to

102

the lay-by and bandaged my eyes. My hands were already tied under my legs. They had done that in the courtyard. It was about forty kilometres to where the road bypassed Piacenza and we turned off before then and drove on for another hour on slow, winding roads. We went up a hill road which got steeper and steeper and when the car stopped it was as hot as an oven.

They left me alone in the car for about ten minutes and then the goon took off the bandage and untied my hands. He jabbed me with his pistol and I stumbled out. There was a sharp pain in my legs as I tried to stand upright. The villa was surrounded on all sides by olive groves and an area of lemon and peach trees. It was white with a red tiled roof that was almost completely hidden by great masses of bougainvillaea. Six brick steps led up to a tiled patio with big red clay pots planted with geraniums and nasturtiums. The front of the building consisted of four archways making a cool, shaded cloister leading to a slatted door and shuttered windows. Inside it had cool marble floors and cast-iron garden furniture painted white, with cupboards, tables and sideboards in dark pine, Abruzzi peasant style. There were various rooms leading off the main room. An old lady in Italian black and a rough-looking young man appeared to be the villa staff.

The girl showed me into a room with a bathroom. Both rooms had barred windows apart from the blue shutters. I heard the girl talking on the telephone in the big room, but I couldn't hear what she was saying. I heard her hang up and then there was the sound of her heels on the marble floor as she walked over to my room. The door was open and as I washed my hands and face in the handbowl she stood in the doorway, watching me. As I towelled my face she spoke. 'It's Max, isn't it?' I nodded.

She walked over and sat on my bed. She leaned back on her elbows. Her long glossy black hair made a stunning contrast to the tan of her face and arms against the fine white woollen dress. She had another strap round her throat. Now it was white linen but the clasp looked the same. She saw me looking at it and she put her head on one side in smiling invitation. I bent down to examine it. The yellow gold was deeply engraved with that bundle of sticks surrounding an axe that goes under the name of 'fasces'. In the time of the Caesars they were carried in front of the senators. Much later they were carried as the symbol of Mussolini's blackshirts. They were banned in public thirty years ago.

'We've got a problem, Max.'

'Oh, what's that, me?'

'No. You booked two airplane seats which you didn't use. We're wondering, why two? Did someone come with you? If so, who? And, if so, why? And, if so, where are they now?'

I smiled. 'That should keep them busy for a time.'

She smiled back. 'The police are checking the hotels and the pensione now.'

And that little kick in the slats was to let me know that they had use of the police whenever they wanted.

She went on. 'They'll be concentrating on the blonde from Santa Margherita. Tammy Walton, wasn't it? She's bound to be registered somewhere.'

They didn't miss a trick, but it'd be a long time before they caught up with Tammy. Signora Mondadori was a match for the Germans as well as the Italians and young Tammy wasn't going on any *questura* register. We'd already decided that.

We ate in mid-evening and I played chess with la Sylva and she took two out of four games. She would have won another but she wasn't used to the odd unorthodox move. Whoever taught her must have been a very strong orthodox player but he hadn't passed on the ability to respond to a spoiling move in a set-piece attack. When we had finished, she poured us a whisky apiece and turned on the tape recorder and the hi-fi and we got nice bits of Telemann, Boccherini and Tartini as a background.

'You married, Max?'

'Way back. Divorced just after the war.'

'Nobody since?'

'Oh yes. Lots of somebodies . . . but no marriage.'

'And you earn enough from the boats?'

'More than enough. My own boat's paid for and I don't need much to live on.'

'We were told you've done a few things apart from the boats. A little job for MI6 in Hanover, kidnapping a boy in Amsterdam who'd been kidnapped by his rich daddy, and a little job in Greece about narcotics.'

I gave her back the smile. 'I like to help when I can.'

'Why?'

'There are times when governments, the police, the establishment or even the law can't do the right thing. Somebody like me can do the washing-up after they've made a mess.'

She stood up, blew me a kiss and said, 'Sleep tight, Max. See you tomorrow.'

No threats about guards or not escaping, but it wasn't really necessary. We were all in the business.

I spent an hour checking the room and the bathroom. The bars on the windows were tough steel and they were embedded about a foot deep in stone top and bottom. They'd take a long time to file or saw through, and they would bend under a heavy hammer but they wouldn't break. The tiles were set on cement and, when I tapped it, it sounded at least eight inches thick. I slowly turned the knob on the door and gently pushed. It was locked. There was hope in the ceiling. It came away slowly to a nail file. It was lath and plaster with reinforcing wire, but the wire was not all that thick. It would take about four or five hours to make a hole big enough to get through but it would be difficult to hide the spoil. And I had no idea what went on on the other side.

I sat and smoked and tried to work out the background. Veronica Page's accountant had probably rumbled the basics of what Dixon was up to. He couldn't prove it in a hundred years but he was keeping his client out of it. A gang could drop its hot money and goods with Dixon. He, or somebody else, financed them for some months. Through his rag-trade business he could shift it overseas whenever they wanted. And for all this the financier and the glorified fence would be making about fifty per cent of the local take. The business had to absorb some of Dixon's take when it began to overflow and that's why it showed such a successful pattern. For some reason the flow had stopped and the business didn't look so good. The armed visit from Dodds was to bring him back into line, the note made that clear. But the initials on the note were those of Signor Timonetti and no stretch of the imagination could make him part of a London armed robbery gang. I couldn't see any credible connection between Dodds and Timonetti. Timonetti was a politician, a man of influence and power, not a crook. And then there was Dixon. I was sure he expected to meet up with Tammy, otherwise sending her to Santa Margherita was pointless. Or was it a smokescreen? But his note to me would have meant including me in the smokescreen. And that smokescreen cost the price of the boat. If he'd double-crossed the London gang in some way, why should he get a note with Timonetti's initials on it? Why should Timonetti know so much about Dixon and why should he be so interested in me? And last, but not least, why hadn't they knocked me off already? There was a possible reason for that. Nobody . . . neither the gang, nor the police in England and Italy, had a pressure on them about Dixon. If somebody took up his disappearance in due course, there would be no reason to suspect murder and in any case the trail would be ice-cold. But Timonetti wasn't sure that my disappearance would go unnoticed. A lot of people might be raising some hell. They weren't sure what I knew and whom I'd talked to. Hence the kid-gloves. For a time I was in baulk, and I was going to stay hard up against the cushion as long as I could. When I started, I had just wanted to make sure I really had 'won' the Fjord. I'd had Dixon's money and the boat was still mine. If he was dead, it was going to stay mine. It was worth even more in Santa Margherita. Maybe I'd do a deal with Timonetti but I didn't really fancy that. I wanted to know why Dixon was killed.

Eight

For two days nothing much happened. I built up a picture of the villa and tested how long my rope was. The girl went off a couple of times but not long enough to have gone to Milan. An additional servant arrived on the third day and it looked as though they were doubling up the guards. I'd seen other men, obviously guards, walking slowly in the fields up the slope behind the villa, and there were two or three who paraded along the rutted path that led down the hill to the road. On the second night my room had not been locked but when I opened it very quietly one of the guards was sitting facing the door with a machine pistol across his lap. They'd done this sort of thing before. The routine looked casual but they were very tight and professional.

The girl would have long chats and I would mark up the questions that were eased in so gently to find out the missing bits. They covered my recent contacts in London, old friends I might have in Milan, Tammy, and that sort of jazz. The kind of stuff you get in SOE at about lesson three on interrogation. You can't plead the Geneva Convention and name, rank and number in Civvy Street, but you can lace a tiny bit of truth they already know with a good mixture of dead ends and false trails. The girl had a very alert mind, bright as a Coke tin, but she hadn't had the training. One thing the questions did tell me. They hadn't struck oil with Tammy. The other good thing was that they clearly saw me as one of the tough lads but they hadn't looked hard enough at the background. If you can cope with the OVRA and the Gestapo, pretty girls with dimples aren't going to be good enough.

On the third day the girl took a phone call just before lunch and, although she didn't say much, I had the feeling that something was wrong. She was getting new orders. We had brandy after lunch and she stretched out her long brown legs and looked at me as she swished her brandy around in the big balloon glass.

'Max, what do you want to know about Dixon?'

'I want to know if he's dead.'

'I've already told you he's dead.'

'And who killed him and why.'

She looked down at her drink. Women do that instinctively when they want to sort out the words when what they're going to say could put them in a bad light and they want to make it sound like it's all your fault. I waited with interest until she looked up.

'He was killed by his associates because he tried to double-cross them.'

'You mean the thieves?'

She took a sip with closed eyes. Another bad sign. She nodded as she put the glass down.

'Yes, it was just a quarrel among thieves.'

'So how do you and Timonetti come into it?'

'We don't, Max; that was a coincidence.'

'With Dino Timonetti's initials on Dodds' little note when he came down to rough up Dixon at Santa Margherita? Come off it, lady.'

She sat up straight in her chair.

'Max, I'd better put you in the picture. We can fix it so that you stand trial for killing Dodds. The young blonde will be an accessory. It would be a long time before you came to trial. At least a year, maybe two. If you drop this ridiculous business of Dixon, Timonetti and his friends will pay you twenty thousand pounds in any currency you want and that will be that.'

I looked at her pretty face and big doe eyes, and for a moment both of us were somewhere else. Her eyelids fluttered and cleared the lines again.

'Why don't your people just kill me like they killed Dixon?'

The anger and frustration showed through as she stood up. She walked to her room and slammed the door.

I ate alone that evening. I had my mind on the phone and I didn't even glance at it until I'd finished. When I looked, it had been unplugged and removed.

I lay awake wondering if I'd gone too far. Maybe it would have been better to look like I'd go along with them. Maybe better still actually to go along. But they were fixers. Fixers with a lot of clout and if I went along I'd end up like Dixon the first chance they got.

I padded round the room but there were no bright thoughts. The door hadn't been locked and I eased it open a couple of inches. There was no guard in sight.

I opened it wider. There was moonlight washing over the white furniture and the tiled floor and no guard. There was the silhouette of a man outside the window and I heard a metallic sound as he shifted his position. I was bending down to check if the phone was back when my head exploded.

When I came to, I tried to remember where I was, but I couldn't move my body or my head and I could just make out white walls and a picture on the wall facing me. Then the waves seemed to cover me over and I felt warm and relaxed as I floated just under the surface. Next time I didn't try so hard and I got better results. I could see the picture. It was a big picture, an oil painting. It was of Sylva Pelozzi wearing the little black band round her throat. Otherwise she was quite naked. The background was plain white canvas and the deeply tanned body was lithe and smooth. Her black hair was like a wild mane and her arms were stretched wide in invitation. The firm breasts looked as if they had been oiled and there were highlights on the taut belly. Her legs were showgirl's legs and the black thatch between them was meticulously painted. She was smiling, and the artist had caught her healthy animal teeth. The dimples were there and their demure effect added its own erotic touch.

I leaned up on one elbow and felt the back of my head. Over behind my right ear was a lump that throbbed and pulsed in a life all its own. It felt as big as a tennis ball so it probably was half that size. Bumps on the head always feel like that. I looked around the room. It was obviously the girl's room and there were lights on in the main room. As I swung my legs off the bed she came in with a bowl on a tray and a towel over her arm. No band at her throat and a man's bathrobe.

'That was silly, Max. Very silly.'

There wasn't a lot of room for argument. She did her Red Cross work on the back of my head and she pressed a button by the bed and one of the outside guards took away the bowl and the towel. It was quite bloody and so was the pillow.

She sat on the bed and looked at me, smiling, but without the superior smirk. Her black hair was switched over one shoulder and it took the eye down to the smooth tops of her breasts. Not that the eye needed assistance. She saw me looking and she opened her mouth to say something, changed her mind and walked over and shut the door. She untied the towelling belt and the bathrobe slid down to her arms. She stood by the bed and as I looked she let the bathrobe go the rest of its journey to the floor. All my instincts told me this was the value added tax on the money deal. Just one instinct said it was no time for tax avoidance. Those cool, calm, elegant girls can be very deceptive with their clothes on and the lovely Sylva was no exception. That soft mouth, the elegant hands and those warm, agile hips worked their lovely wonders with an enthusiasm that only a churl could have ignored. And churl I never was.

When I awoke it was ten o'clock. I was in the girl's bed but there was no sign of her. Nobody stopped me when I walked across to my room. The old lady came in with coffee and rolls. There was talking and some laughing from the kitchen and everyone seemed suddenly relaxed.

113

A young man, one of the guards, came in and said it was permitted that I walk outside if I wished, and he would be my escort.

In the bright sunlight my eyes had to squint and it was not easy to walk. There was a big spread of mimosa and I sat on the slope and looked at the panorama. There was an occasional flash from a car windscreen far over the flat plain, and small clusters of houses that must have made up the villages that lined the country roads to the autostrada. There was a magnificent view but no reference points. I'd sat for half an hour before the guard spoke.

'Signor.'

'Yes.'

He spoke softly, almost a whisper. 'You were *capitano* in the war, yes?'

'That's right.'

'You remember a Gino del Rossi?'

I turned and looked up at him, surprised

'I remember him very well.'

'He my father.'

I patted the grass beside me and he sat down a few feet away.

'What's he doing now?'

'He is carpenter in Piacenza and mayor of our small town.'

'Still a Marxist?'

He laughed and nodded. 'Yes. Now more than ever.'

'You must be the new baby, Ernesto.'

'No, I am the next one, Angelo.'

'Does he speak of those days?'

The young man laughed. 'He never stops, signor. My

mama says we fight with the partisans every time we eat.'

'He was a brave man, Angelo.'

The boy nodded and his eyes avoided mine. 'I tell him about you and he not like it much.'

'You tell him I can look after myself, boy.'

He was silent for a few moments, his fingers pulling at the sparse grass. 'He say I to help you, signor.'

I turned to look at him. 'And what do you say?'

'I do as he say, signor.'

'What happens when they find out?'

He grinned. 'They not find out, signor.'

We spent half an hour on planning and he briefed me on the roads and conditions. It was going to be that night. I spent an hour bolting on my own variations. It could be a set-up where I'm the thief who gets shot while robbing the gentry's villa. It didn't have that kind of smell but I was always cautious when my leathery hide might get another hole or stripe.

The girl didn't show up at all that day. Not even for the evening meal. I slept for a couple of hours with my clothes on. Just before two I opened the door quietly. Angelo was guarding the front of the house and the goon was sitting in the armchair in the main room. His chin was on his chest and his head nodded from time to time as he fought off sleep. My bare feet seemed to make a hell of a noise as they kept peeling off the tiles with each step. When I was right behind him, he heard something and half turned. I went the other way and as my hand went over his mouth his big hands grabbed my arm. My other thumb went behind his left ear and found the little slot between his skull and his jaw and, as he struggled to get up, I bore down on him and pressed, deep and hard. He cried out but my hand muffled the sound. His body shuddered massively and then went limp. I pressured him for another thirty seconds. Just to the borders of being lethal.

I lifted the Luger and pulled back the slide. There was a round up the spout and it flew out almost to the door. The slide picked up the next round and it slammed into the barrel. It took several minutes to find the ejected round and I slipped it into my pocket. Outside the shuttered door was Angelo and as he turned I slammed my fist and it took him on the chin. I caught him as he fell and laid him in the shadows of the patio. The moon was full and I made my way carefully down the brick steps and along the edge of the sloping path. After ten minutes I was way down the hill and, when I left the path to make for the road, I saw lights go on in the villa and I could hear faint shouts. Ten minutes later I heard a motorcycle start and I lay among the rocks and watched it coming down the path. When it went past I saw that there was a man on the pillion clinging to the driver. He was swinging a torch each side of the path as they bumped their way down. I had reckoned that anyone looking for me would go up towards Milan to cut me off, so when I moved on I headed south towards Piacenza. I was going to wait for the light. With traffic on the autostrada it would cover my noise. At night they could wait and listen and when they heard me they had me.

A kilometre from the autostrada the hill was less steep and there were cypresses in clusters and I made for the largest clump. It was already four and birds were rustling and chirping sporadically as I moved into the trees. I found a small flat clearing and settled down to wait for the day to come. As I waited I thought of the boat, and I could almost hear the slap of water on her hull as some early-bird boat locked out from the pool to Chichester channel and the Solent. There must be something wrong with men who don't settle down with a wife, two kids, a garden, a mortgage, a season ticket and a pension.

I played it safe and waited until ten o'clock and then went down to the southbound track of the autostrada. There was a greengrocer's lorry in the first lay-by and he dropped me in the via Scalabrini and I took the country bus to del Rossi's little village. I got off at the piazza and there was an old lady waiting at the bus-stop. I asked her how I could find Gino del Rossi. The old lady looked up at me and, as she shuffled away, she said, 'Gino del Rossi *e morto. Cinque anni fa.*'

By instinct alone I turned round and got back on the bus. I had only enough money for the fare to the next village and one telephone call. I sat on the hot seat and looked through the dusty window. They *had* set it up. And it had almost worked. I could have headed back to Milan and they'd have trailed me to Tammy. Watched me for a few days to check on my contacts and Tammy and I would have made a small paragraph in the *Corriere della Sera* when they found us. British couple murdered in Milan shanty-town mystery, police chief warns tourists to keep to central areas after dark. The bastards: they'd put up the money deal, then the girl had done her bit, then they dug the hole for me

117

to drop into. Instinct took me in the opposite direction but I'd been stupid. You can afford that kind of stupidity only once every five years. I wondered what Gino del Rossi thought from his grave of the son who sold the Englishman down the river. He'd probably have approved, and that thought, for some peculiar reason, cheered me up.

The bus ground to a stop in a cloud of dust and I looked around for signs of a tail. I was the only one who got off and the few people in the square were obviously locals going about their business. There was the Ristorante di Genova or the Albergo Emmanuelle. I headed for the restaurant and phoned Mario at his office. He was in.

'Max, where are you?'

'Mario, it may be best you don't know. I want some things.'

'OK.'

'I want two hundred pounds in lire and a passport.'

'There's no British Consul here, Max. The nearest is Genova and they'll need to see you personally. I've done it before and it's a hell of a game.'

'I don't want *my* passport, Mario. Just get me a passport. British, American, Irish, anything.'

There was a long pause and a sigh for the troublesome *Inglesi*.

'I can get you an Irish one. What about the photograph?'

'Forget it. They never look at that in hotels. That's all I want it for.'

'Where is this to go to?'

'Mail me the money to the post office here. It's a

dump called Borgio. Put the passport for me *fermo
posta* at the central post office in Milan, the one on the
via Marconi. I shall need it tonight, Mario.'

'Max, they are watching me in case you come here.
They have been watching ever since you left.'

'Don't worry, Mario. Can you do the passport by
tonight?'

'Yes, I've got it in the safe. Only six months to go
before it is invalid.'

'That's fine. Bye, Mario,' and I hung up.

I ordered coffee, rolls and some peaches and I sat
for two hours reading *La Stampa*. I'd read through it
once and had a go at the crossword without a pen or
pencil. It was only when I'd ordered another coffee and
was folding up the paper so that the girl could wipe
the table that I saw it, right on the front page and right
in the middle:

At a rally held in Milan last night Signor Dino
Timonetti announced a break-away group from the
Moviemento Sociale Italiano. Signor Timonetti, the
well-known industrialist, said that he and other
members had long felt that the MSI was not
adhering to the party's programme as laid down
in the 1972 manifesto, particularly with regard to
new laws to control the trades unions and the reduc-
tion or elimination of vatican privileges. Observers
have suggested that the timing of the announce-
ment coincided with a secret agreement with
communist party interests on future action in many
spheres.

Signor Timonetti and other leaders of the new

party are meeting in Rome this coming weekend and it is rumoured that senior military commanders will also attend in a private capacity. The new party is to be called La Bandiera Nera and temporary offices have been established in the Via Mangoni.

Readers will remember that the Milan police have been investigating the Milan branch of the MSI in connection with the series of explosions which occured in January and February. No report has yet been issued and a spokesman for the police stated that the investigations were proceeding normally.

Local officials of the MSI have so far refused to comment on the new group but a spokesman for the Christian Democrats claimed that the new group were 'fascists in a hurry'. It was expected in government circles in Rome that foreign opinion might be alarmed by this new development in the already delicate political situation in this country.

The white jigsaw was beginning to get some picture in it. The break-away party was almost certainly why they were going easy on me. But it was also the reason why my escape would harden them up. I had a sneaky feeling that somehow Dixon's death was linked with the new party, not politically but in some important way. For me it was time to bow out. Dixon was dead. I could keep the boat. Whatever Timonetti was up to, he could get on with it as far as I was concerned.

The money was there at the post office but I had a deal of talking to do. They didn't want to hand it over without identification from my passport. At the end of ten minutes' fruitless argument I had a brainwave. I took off my watch and slid off the wristband. Engraved on the back it said, 'Capitano Farne – Croce di Guerra – Partigiani 195 – Ottobre 1943.' And it was good enough.

There were two taxis in Borgio and I hired the good one. It was a 1940 Lancia Aprillia. The one where the gear lever comes off every third time you used it. The driver could drive, talk non-stop and screw the gear lever back without looking. He'd once done a record hire to Piacenza but this time it was the story of his life. All the way to Milan. He'd come from Sicily just after the war and lived in the stinking shanty-town on the outskirts of Milan. But in five years he'd become a skilled car mechanic. He had married a girl from Piacenza and they'd lived in Borgio for thirteen years. Now he was his own master. When we had completed his saga I asked him what he thought of the new party. He leaned back in the driving seat and whistled and made that little chopping motion with his hand that expresses the Italian working man's ability to be shocked and impressed at the same time.

'He's a big big man, that Timonetti. He and those others, I tell you, they're more Fascist than Musso. Everyone expected them to break away six weeks ago. That's what the newspapers said at the time.'

'What do they want to do that the MSI doesn't do?'

He laughed. 'Not much, really, but they want to do it right now. The MSI have been talking too long – nobody believes them any more. Timonetti and his pals have got the police and the army on their side. Remember what Mussolini used to say, "Better a year as a lion than a century as sheep." That's these fellows today. Everybody's sick of inflation and the priests and strikes and the rich, and they'll listen to anybody who says they'll finish it in a couple of months.'

'Why the agreement with the Communists?'

He shrugged with both hands off the wheel. 'They need one another, signor. Each one thinks he is using the other.'

When we got to the outskirts of Milan I made his day and told him to go round the ring road and come in from the east. He was enraptured when he saw the new airport at Forlanini and I got him to drop me by the big garage on the Viale Cornica. He was still blowing kisses as he did an illegal U-turn and headed back for Borgio, home and beauty.

I took a bus to the central station and walked to the post office. There was a thick packet for me and I went through the watch routine again. I told him my passport was at the hotel. He asked the name of the hotel and that seemed to satisfy him. I bought slacks and two shirts and had a meal. It was almost eight o'clock. The passport photograph was nothing like me so it had at least that touch of authenticity. It was in the name of Sean Burke, which didn't sound all that Irish to me. He was three years younger than me. I checked the flight arrival times from London and twenty minutes later I booked in at a hotel in one of the small streets off the viale Brianza. I bathed and shaved and phoned down to the porter for a paper, a hired TV, and a bottle of Coronata. Tomorrow I'd contact Signora Mondadori and arrange to meet Tammy at the airport. Tomorrow or the day after we'd be on the boat at Chichester. I'd get Mario to flog the Fjord at Santa Margherita. We'd have a week or two at Chichester and then we'd head for Honfleur and make our way round the French coast and have a month's cruising in the Bay of Morbihan. I'd learned not to get hooked on a particular girl but I liked young Tammy and I liked what she let me do. We'd see how it went.

On TV there was half an hour of highlights from Juventus playing a friendly against Atletico. There were no goals, forty-five fouls and a lot of good acting. Then we got the news. A report from the EEC ministers in Brussels on regional payments, with honourable special mention of north-east England and southern Italy. An Alitalia flight had narrowly avoided a light plane when landing at Fiumicino. Then we saw Dino Timonetti arriving in Rome for important meetings. The hawk-like face was thrust forward aggressively and his comments on the government were bitter and provoca-tive. Smiling and cheering supporters jostled to touch him as police cleared a way for his triumphant depart-ure. The Italian fleet was given a warm welcome as it arrived in Taranto from NATO exercises. There was a cheerful interview with a hundred-year-old lady from Naples and I was just leaning forward to switch off the set when there was a hand-held shot of a street I recog-nized, then a doorway I recognized. There were *cara-binieri* holding back a small crowd as a stretcher was manoeuvred down the steps towards the back of an ambulance. A weeping Signora Mondadori was escorted to a police car. The voice-over reported the murder of an English girl tourist in mysterious circumstances. The proprietress of the pensione was making a statement to the police. The name of the murdered girl had not yet been released by the police.

All the exhaustion of the day poured through me, and my heart thumped wildly as my hands gripped the wooden arms of the chair. All the cockiness, all the self-confidence evaporated. I felt as if I were made of stone, cold and inert. Then the hot anger suffused me and my fists ached for something to smash. Something human, something Italian. The bastards couldn't wait to see what I would do. When they lost me, they had to teach me a lesson. They'd killed the girl cold-bloodedly, mercilessly. No threats, no deals. Just zap and she was dead. Wherever I was, I'd get the message.

I wasn't conscious of the crowds in the evening streets. I needed to walk, to walk fast, and I found myself in the Piazza del Duomo. There was flood-lighting on the cathedral and the gothic arches threw up fountains of cool stone that spurted skywards to be frozen in finials and lace-work that hung in delicate traceries of worship. I walked slowly across the square past the looped chains that held off the streams of cars. There were scarlet cloths hanging on the doors and a workman's wicker basket hung against a spire. Without knowing it, this was what had brought me here. A small door was open in the big bronze door and I went in. The lights were yellow and orange and the vaulted roof was in shadow. Fat yellow candles were alight and wavering each side of the aisle. I sat in one of the seats reserved for invalids and I bent my head for peace. Finding no peace, I prayed. The distorted, terrible prayers of those who only pray when desperate. I prayed for Tammy Walton and promised impossible things if only she could be made happy. I prayed for myself and finally abused the building and its God by begging his help in killing Dino Timonetti. There was no balm for me that night and I left as wild-eyed as I came.

There was no sleep either and I lay on the bed in the strange room trying not to think of Tammy surprised by her attackers and then frightened and pleading as they killed her. I didn't know how she had died so my nightmare mind played havoc in my head. I must have slept until about six and I awoke with a start as the waiter knocked and brought in coffee and rolls and the morning paper. There were two or three paragraphs on an inside page. They gave her name and that her body was being flown back to England today. Mr James Bravington, a stockbroker and her stepfather, had made arrangements with the British Consul. The Milan police were continuing their inquiries. A post-mortem showed that she died from extensive knife wounds. And nobody said they were sorry.

I bathed and shaved and sat in the comfortable chair and tried to work out what to do. Timonetti must have had all my contacts from partisan days investigated in the effort to close the net round me and to find out who had come with me from England. And suddenly, as I worked it out, a whole piece of jigsaw fell into place. It had been there all the while and I'd forgotten it. I'd asked Mavis Travers if D.T. was the boss and she'd said 'yes'. So there *was* a link between the gang of armed robbery experts and Timonetti. Why? What possible use would they have for each other?

Nine

On the midday news they said that the police were looking for an Englishman in connection with the murder of the girl tourist in Milan. They gave no name but a reasonably accurate description of me. Timonetti's boys weren't wasting any time. The police would be watching the stations and the airports.

There was a man in Milan I wanted to contact. Gianni Podoni. Gianni Podoni was a crook. He was born in Naples and he'd thieved and pimped from the age of ten. When I first knew him he was twenty-four and he had come up from La Spezia with two of his men for sten guns and ammunition. Even then he was big, ugly in an attractive sort of way, and making money. But his partisan group had a record of success against the Germans that reflected a ruthlessly capable organizer. Men twice his age carried out his orders as if they came from the good Lord himself. He was a born leader and a born crook. By the time the Italians became co-belligerents in 1943 he had a well-organized black market network operating all over northern Italy. In early 1944 he was picked up by MilGov and prosecuted. No Italian lawyer would defend him against the righteous wrath of MilGov. Round about that time the War Office dreamed up a special leave called Python for all their soldier-boys who had languished in Cairo for the last two years. So I claimed my Python leave and took it on myself, with some unofficial hand-holding from a mate in the Judge Advocate's department. After three weeks it wasn't clear whether they were prosecuting Gianni or me, and they called it a day. There's nothing more soul-destroying for a competent lawyer than to carry a case for weeks on end against a bloody-minded amateur who doesn't give a damn for the law or the court. They had one more go at him, this time for organizing prostitution in Firenze. I was back in London waiting to go to Germany and I contacted Florence Sub-Area and offered a list of names that the defence would subpoena, and they called it a day. None of it took all that much effort. They turned down the second DSO recommendation, and Gianni offered me a partnership in his thriving conglomerate of crookery. I'd seen him two or three times since the war and he was the same happy rogue but his organization was more formal and his clothes were custom-made. So were the girls.

The last time I had met him was in a superb apartment on the via Torino. So I checked with the telephone operator but there was no number listed for any Podonis except a bottling plant for a cola drink, and that was way out between Monza and Lecco. I spoke to the General Manager. Yes, Signor Podoni was the owner and president but he only visited for monthly meetings, and no, he couldn't give me a home telephone number. Or if he could he wasn't going to. When I asked him if Podoni still lived on the via Torino, the pause was just long enough for me to know he was still there. If the police were watching all my old contacts, they'd be watching the via Torino for sure.

There is a café opposite the church in the via Torino and I ate there watching Gianni's block. There were two *carabinieri* each side of the main entrance chatting to the doorman. It was a no parking area and right outside the main doors was a white Lincoln convertible whose opulent extravagance stank of my friend Gianni.

When the waiter was refilling my coffee I asked him if he knew Gianni Podoni's apartment. He shook his head.

'No, signor. Never heard of him.'

I suppose there must be somebody in Milan who actually hadn't heard of Gianni Podoni. But this guy wasn't the one. I counted out five 1,000 lire notes and folded them over.

'I want you to take him a message. OK?'

'Tha's OK, signor. You got the note?'

'It's not a note. Just a message.'

'OK, signor.'

'Just say, "*Io voglio fischiatar*". And tell him where I am. If the cops ask any questions, you're answering Signor Podoni's telephone call. Taking an order for food. Understand? And when you come back, serve somebody else before you speak to me.'

He nodded and went off to get his jacket and I watched him walk across the street. The *carabinieri* didn't speak to him. Just nodded as he went past them up the steps.

Back in 1944 there'd been an Ensa party giving a show in Firenze for the troops and the local Italians. There'd been a very pretty girl singer who must wonder to this day why she brought the house down. There was a nice little ditty from *Snow White and the Seven Dwarfs* called 'Whistle While You Work', and some diligent impresario had cobbled together a verse in Italian with the aid of a dictionary. Nobody'd told him that in Italian the word for whistling had another more exciting meaning, and when the pretty girl sang '*Io voglia fischiatar*' – 'All I want to do is whistle' – there was a split second of silence and then a roar of Italian applause that must have made her feel she was getting her first taste of Hollywood stardom. None had clapped louder than our Gianni.

It was nearly twenty minutes before the waiter came back and while he was hanging up his jacket I saw Gianni come down the steps. He was with a girl and another man. The doorman stood holding open the car door while Gianni laughed with the *carabinieri*. The big white Lincoln drove off with its rear wheels spinning and grit flying. The waiter didn't come near me, but five minutes later a taxi pulled up and the driver got out, took a look around and then headed for me.

'Signor Podoni says you come with me.'

We drove sedately down the Corso Ponte Romana and then into a network of side streets where it joins the Corso Lodi. I noticed that we passed the fruit-market and then dived under the autostrada. Just past the Ponte Lambro I saw the white Lincoln in the lights of the taxi and we pulled over to the side of the road just in front. Gianni was standing there waiting and he pulled open the taxi door and clambered in. The big paw reached for my hand before he sat down.

'My God, Max, this is wonderful! What the hell are you doing over here? Why all the secret service stuff?'

'I'm in trouble, Gianni. Real trouble.'

The big ugly face broke into a grin.

'Great, marvellous. What can I do?'

'The police are after me, Gianni.'

He laughed and his big crooked teeth were still the same.

'That's no worry, *ragazzo*. I soon fix that. What they want you for?'

'They want me for murder, Gianni.'

With anyone else you'd need to establish in ten seconds that it wasn't true and that you hadn't done it. But not with Gianni.

'So what. Who was it, *amico*?'

'You'd better hold on. It's more than that. I've got crossed up with a guy named Timonetti.'

The little piggy eyes narrowed slightly but the grin stayed put. He was a professional now. He slapped his leg and laughed.

'That's my boy. Always picks the big ones. What's it all about?'

I gave him a ten-minute run-down and he asked a few questions. He was silent for a few minutes and when he spoke I guessed he needed more time to think.

'Where you holed up now?' And I told him.

'OK, you go back with this driver. He waits for you while you pick up your things and check out. Then he bring you to my place.'

'What about the *carabinieri*?'

He laughed, and it was like the MGM lion.

'Not to worry, boy. I fix those dumb bastards OK.'

He reached for the door handle and turned towards me.

'Is great to see you, Max. Everything I've got I give you.' For a moment I thought he was going to give me a kiss like Juventus strikers get when the ball goes in the net. He hesitated, then laughed and got out.

I gathered up my kit at the hotel and checked out. We drove back to the via Torino. The *carabinieri* were not in evidence and the taxi driver walked up the steps with me. Sitting in a white spindly chair was a pretty girl who looked up as I went through the swing doors. She checked me over with her eyes and then got up smiling. 'Signor Max?' I nodded.

'Gianni's waiting for you.'

We went up to the seventeenth floor and along a corridor. The girl pressed the bell twice and a man opened the door. He was dressed exactly like a mythical English butler.

'Good evening, sir. May I take your bag?' He *was* an English butler. And he showed no dismay at taking over two dirty shirts and my old faded jeans. The girl waited, smiling, as we made the handover. Then she took me down a small passage and opened a door.

'This is your apartment, Signor. Signor Podoni will be along in a minute.'

The apartment had a large living room, a double bedroom and a bathroom. The décor was restful and modern and there was a radio, television, and drinks and food in a refrigerator in the small hallway. I soaked in a hot bath and when Gianni came in he sat on the toilet seat and flicked his cigarette ash into the hand-basin.

'I've sent a man to the Napoleone to do a quiet check. The police have got your passport so that will relax them a bit. I've put a man out checking what has happened at Mama Mondadori's place. Timonetti's still in Rome, but will be back tomorrow night. The police have been instructed to arrest you and remove you to Torino into the care of a Capitano Farese. He's one of Timonetti's stooges.'

'What have they got in mind?'

He grinned. 'If it works out nicely, they kill you. If there are problems, they will hold you incommunicado in Torino and maybe put you on trial.'

'But I can prove I wasn't in Milan when Tammy was killed.'

'You think Timonetti and his boys will testify that you were held prisoner, *amico*? Never.'

'Why do they care about me so much anyway?'

'Because you could destroy the new party – La Bandiera Nera.'

'Me! I don't give a damn one way or the other.'

He smiled. 'You don't know half the story, Max. But they don't know that.'

'You'd better tell me.'

He nodded. 'Sure I tell you but not tonight. You need a rest. But tell me what have you got in mind. You like to go to London tomorrow? I can do that easily. No trouble.'

I put my feet up on the taps and Gianni watched my face as I was thinking.

'I'd rather stay. But it's up to you.'

'Max, I owe you everythin' I have. My money, my people, my influence, they are yours to use.'

'Even against Timonetti?'

'Even against my best friend, Max. There is no limit.'

And none of it was said with a flourish. It was just a plain, businesslike statement of fact.

'You like the little girl who brought you up here? She pretty for you?'

'Very pretty, Gianni, but I'll be glad of a real sleep. But thanks for the offer, if it was an offer.'

He laughed. 'Sure it was an offer. There are plenty more when you're ready.'

It was midday before I awoke and Gianni was sitting in one of the big leather chairs reading the paper. He was wearing a blue cotton shirt and blue slacks. He looked fresh and alert and I felt tired and tatty. He looked across at me and then pressed a button at the end of the bed.

'*Ciao*, Max, how you feel? They're gonna bring you some breakfast. Then we talk.'

He waited till I was dressed before he started.

'How much you know about Timonetti, Max?'

'He's rich, important and influential. That's about it.'

'Influential, yes. The other two things, no. That's a con. He's from a good family. Comes from Livoru. They were merchants. Dino was an enthusiastic Fascist, built himself an independent business building houses, schools and so on. This was when he was just a kid. Then came the war. He was a *capitano* in the Engineers. Served in the colonies. Somalia and Ethiopia. Taken prisoner by your people in Mogadiscio. Was smuggled back to Italy on one of those hospital ships that repatriated civilians. Was transferred to the police and promoted. Then bang. We were out of the war. Your people and the Provisional Government put the grip on all the enthusiastic *fascisti* and Timonetti was clobbered. No job, no money, no influence, no family. He worked on a petrol pump for some time and somebody put the word in and he lost even that job. There were a lot of others in the same boat. There were a lot of old scores settled at that time. So you'd got a lot of people who knew their way around with no hope and no prospects and they quietly got together. Timonetti operated on the black market. Made a living, not much more, but slowly it all settled down. The war was over, everybody started settling back and forgetting, except Timonetti and his friends. They worked with the Communists and they began to have influence. They couldn't change anything. Couldn't make things happen. But they could stop things happening. They put people where it mattered. In the police, in the army, in ministries and so on. Nobody did anything about them. Nobody thought they mattered and some people thought they'd had a raw deal anyway.

'Timonetti stayed outside everything. Lots of influence but no money. People gave him money to live on but it was peanuts. Then it was fixed with somebody in one of the ministries and he started getting bribe money for fixing import and export licences. And, if you were a foreigner selling things in Italy, you wanted an import licence. Somehow you never got it till you got together with Dino, and then you were in business. He was a smart operator, that boy. Some of these firms haven't got large sums to pay out. They don't even know that they're going to make that many bucks in Italy anyway. So Dino takes part of the action plus just a little bit of money. Some of them do very well and it's great. Except Dino is always there sitting on their windpipes. He can bring it all to a stop and maybe they go bust. You get the picture now?'

'Is that what happened with Dixon?'

'Sure, Dixon was small-time. Started doing well here through Dino. Needed more dollars to expand and started fencing for those crooks. The money and the stuff came here and Dino disposed of it, taking another cut on the way. In the end, Dino was controlling Dixon and the gang. It was more dangerous that way but he got plenty of protection here because he was pouring that money into his political group. Then Dixon needs more money for his business and I can guess what happens. He keeps a pile. Doesn't ship it out here. Dino puts on the pressure, says he'll stop his business. Dixon probably thinks he can persuade Dino to give him a break. But he's picked the wrong time. Dino's boys are just about to go public with the new party. They need all the money they can get and they don't want anybody rocking the boat. I'd guess Dixon does one more stupid thing. He not only hangs on to the loot and diverts it into his company, but he kids himself that he can come over here and reason with Timonetti or even threaten to tell the world what's been going on. Maybe he could have got away with it, who knows. Timonetti sends the guy down to Santa Margherita to rough up Dixon and that makes me think he hadn't yet decided to finish him. I think maybe one of the London end put out a contract on Dixon and he got killed because there was no other link between them and Timonetti.'

'And now?'

'And now Timonetti is scared you'll expose it all. New Fascist party based on bribery, theft, and corruption.'

'Would the public believe me? Would it do any damage?'

Gianni laughed and shook his head.

'That's not the point, *ragazzo*. The Bandiera Nera party have only just started. Two weeks from now they plan a big *raggiungiamento* in Roma and the big bomb they drop there is the details of bribery and corruption in the Christian Democrat party. Everybody knows it goes on but these boys will have the names. You just think, *ragazzo*, the Christian Democrats are the Vatican's boys and they're caught with their hands in the till. Timonetti gets all the Fascist votes, the Communist votes and a few angry CD votes as well. He's got it made. And then you come wandering around putting your big feet all over the place. Striking matches to find where the gas leak is.'

He sighed and looked across at me, the patient professor with the dim student.

'So what do you want to do, Max?'

'I want to square things off with Timonetti.'

Gianni looked judicial and then stood up, stretching his arms wide.

'He's put a couple of hoods on your boat at Santa Margherita. You'd better bear that in mind. You want to get Timonetti himself or have a go at the Bandiera Nera?'

'What do you feel about them?'

He pursed his lips and shrugged.

'They don't matter to me one way or the other. They won't want to play games with me. I pay my way with whoever is in power.'

'They all take bribes?'

'Sure. It's best that way. You want something or you want something done, OK, you know who you got to pay and how much. If you have your system, nothing gets done; you wait around for committees to decide and you get alongside politicians and if you pick the wrong lot you get stuck for good. Here, they play at being politicians and we get on with our business. Whoever's in power, you pay them. Simple. You want Timonetti. OK, my boys get him for you. No trouble, *amico*.'

'I want to do it, Gianni.'

He shook his head. 'That would be stupid, *amico*. You let us do it. You can send flowers.'

'I still want to do it.'

Gianni walked over to the window and looked out, leaning against the window frame. Then he turned and waved me over. At the window he nodded for me to look too.

We looked across red tiled roofs a hundred years old and then suddenly at the golden white stone of the cathedral shimmering in the sun. More roofs, a few modern blocks and then the Alps, so high they looked as if they were on the edge of the city; they spread across the whole of our view. There were deep blue foothills, pale blue slopes, and then white sparkling snow on the crests, which opened to reveal a valley and peaks that were all snow till they reflected the sky and melted together in a smoky haze. As I looked, Gianni put his hand on my shoulder.

'We fix Timonetti together. You and me.'

I didn't see Gianni again until we ate early in the evening. We took our meal in his apartment and the butler served us as we talked. Gianni obviously had no fear that anyone in his organization would talk.

'How much did you know already about Timonetti's London connections?' I asked him.

'Not very much. The word had gone round that he was servicing a well-organized group in London but nothing more. It wouldn't interest anybody here unless he started working this game in Italy. When I checked on his set-up yesterday, I got a lot more of course.' He gazed across the table at me and his face had a serious look. 'What I don't like is that there's a lot of ex-OAS money and people in with him. There are French Algerians training Timonetti's boys right now. The word is that they did the bomb job in Verona last month, so you've got Fascists planting bombs that kill Fascists to make the public hate the Commies. It's bloody crazy the more I look into it.'

'How well do you know Timonetti?'

'I've met him several times. I've paid him for several things my people wanted.'

'Who supplies the arms for them?'

'Not me, *amico*, not me. Arms, drugs – that's not my business.' He grinned as he chewed on some celery. 'Black market, thieving, girls and gambling, that's my business. I've got a lot of legitimate businesses too. Like the bottling plant.'

'Any ideas on how we tackle Timonetti?'

He shook his head slowly, his eyes on my face, and then he smiled. 'You tell me, *amico*.'

'I want him to watch it fall apart before we fix him. I want him to know that it's me . . . that it's because of Tammy.'

'So?'

'So I want a contact with the press. Just a little bit honest, if that's possible.'

He shrugged. 'Little bit honest we don't find. What we find is a pro-Christian Democrat journalist. Cheaper and surer that way. We'll send the word out and see who takes the bait.'

'Have we got enough to interest him?'

'Sure we have. But we don't mention your Tammy at this stage and we don't meet him here. You meet him on your own, but my boys will be around in case there's any problem.'

'Who's Timonetti's girl?'

Gianni looked almost shocked.

'Timonetti's girl? No such thing, *amico*. Timonetti's girls are boys. You got it wrong someway.'

'Sylva Pelozzi.'

'Jesus! That whore. She comes from a very good family. Close to the old king. She was down at Cine-Città, had a screen test and got a firm contract. She was the mistress of one of the independent producers, got screwed by every bum in the place and was chucked out. Timonetti took her on as a cover for the young boys and to service passing politicians. She service you, *amico*?'

''Fraid so.'

'Ah well, we can do better than that for you.'

The phone rang and Gianni listened and grunted from time to time. It took nearly twenty minutes. When he hung up he said, 'Timonetti and his gang got back to Milan tonight. Very pleased with themselves. He's giving a press conference right now. Calling for new elections. Says the middle parties have been in power too long, that they are ineffective and just play musical chairs with the ministries, taking it in turns. Says the music's gonna stop right now. Trouble is, the bastard's right. Tomorrow we make plans.'

When he was at the door seeing me out he said, 'You ready for a girlfriend yet?'

I shook my head and smiled. He put his hand on my arm. 'You liked that young blonde.' I nodded and walked back to my rooms. It would be a long time before I got young Tammy out of my system.

Ten

The restaurant was a long, rambling structure in white stucco, set back from the road in pleasure gardens. We arrived just before midday. It was just outside Como but not the kind of place that tourists frequented. Gianni got them to fix a table for us in the garden, and the Lincoln had been left in Milan. The small Fiat was tucked in the proprietor's garage. Two of Gianni's men were roaming around the place and they'd got the kind of eyes that didn't miss a thing.

Gianni was as taut as a harp-string, which tends to be normal when you're working on your own home ground. But when the man was shown over to our table he relaxed and we ordered a meal. In England we wouldn't have got down to the business in hand until we got to the coffee, but when the scampi came Gianni plunged in. The journalist was a freelancer and like many journalists he was a visual disappointment. He was a bit over medium height, thin, with round shoulders that emphasized his narrow face and weak chin. His soft brown eyes looked mournful over his drooping modish moustache, and his long delicate fingers were stained from tobacco tar. Gianni had introduced him with respect as Paolo Guarini, and the young man had looked at the table as if the sight of me might offend some journalists' ethic. Gianni painted the background and waited for a response.

Guarini lit a cigarette carefully and slowly, screwing up his eyes from the smoke, and waved out the match as though it were the Olympic torch and slid it back in the box like old soldiers do. Only then did he look across at me.

'You can give the details of the robberies concerned?'

'Yes.'

'And names of the people involved?'

'Some of them, not all of them.'

He reached inside his jacket and sorted through some envelopes, made a few scribbles and then looked up.

'Give me the places and incidents first, and then the names.' He bothered about the spelling and practised the English pronunciation.

'The villa these people took you to. Can you describe it and where it was?'

I went through the routine of what I had seen.

'Where's the note that was signed D.T.?'

'The police have it with the rest of my things, I guess. They took my stuff from the Napoleone.'

'Which police station?'

I shook my head and Gianni chipped in. 'They were at the Centrale, but they may have been shuffled over to Torino.'

Then he gave me a long. languid look as if weighing up the facts so far.

'And what's your interest in Signor Timonetti?'

'I'm interested in anyone who kills my girls.'

He nodded. 'Revenge then. Nothing more?'

'That's it.'

'And you fear that Timonetti might have you killed to keep you quiet?'

'That's one way of putting it.'

He smiled a very small fleeting smile as he looked at his watch, and then said as he looked up at me, 'You look pretty tough, Signor Farne.' When I didn't reply he moved on, 'You were the officer who defended Signor Podoni at the end of the war?'

'Yes.'

'Why did you do that?'

'He was a friend.'

'And you, Signor Podoni? Is it because of that that you are helping this gentleman now?'

Gianni grinned. 'Of course not. I just want my countrymen to be properly informed.'

Guarini didn't smile.

'And what do you expect me to do with this information?'

Gianni banged down a big flat hand on the table.

'Paolo, I chose you because you won't be afraid of Timonetti, and you're a good journalist. We leave it up to you.'

'And if I do nothing?'

'I'll know Timonetti's going to be the next President of the Republic, my boy.'

Guarini smoked with both elbows on the table, eyes screwed up, and he pushed his glasses back up his nose with his thumb. He coughed from time to time as he meditated. Then he looked across at Gianni. 'OK,

145

Signor Podoni. I'll do some checking first. If it checks out, I'll push it around.'

Gianni nodded without looking either pleased or grateful. He wiped his mouth with the back of his hand and leaned back.

'You know where to contact me, Paolo, if you want anything more.' And then he stood up. 'When will it happen?'

Guarini stood up too, and smiled.

'Quite quickly, Gianni. Quite quickly.'

We stayed at the restaurant until the evening, and it was nearly midnight when we got back to the via Torino. On the table in Gianni's room was a large-scale map and I looked at it while Gianni found us each a whisky. Almost in the centre of the map was Timonetti's villa. The 'L' shape and the contours and paths identified it. There was a red-ink line that seemed to mark out the boundaries of the estate. Gianni handed me the drink and then leaned over the map.

'I've got some photographs of the villa coming tomorrow and I've got a man drawing a plan of the villa itself. It's best we settle with Timonetti down there. If we do it in Milan it'll look political and that means his group will keep raising hell about it. Out at the villa we can make it look personal. But it's best to wait a couple of days and see what Paolo does. If the story starts leaking, it's going to put friend Dino off-balance. He'll be looking for a chance to get rough and he won't know how you've done it or who's backing you. He won't think of me till he's tried everything else. He'll be heading for the Christian Democrats first, or the

146

Commies. We'll get him out to the villa and then he's yours. I've got a man checking in Piacenza on his routine when he goes out there.'

We finished our drinks and I went off to my room. On the table at the side of the bed were that day's English papers, the *Daily Express* and *The Times*. Something for everybody. And there was a leather-bound book of a size that indicated culture and coffee tables. I didn't open it until I was undressed and sitting on the bed. On each page was the photograph of a girl. There were twenty, all naked and all beautiful. On the left hand pages were their measurements and their specialities. Some of the specialities I hadn't even heard of. There was quite a bit of Latin amongst the Italian and Latin always seems to add a touch of respectability to way-out sex. I gave them marks out of twenty and the lowest was eighteen. I closed the book and put it back on the table. My two blue-green sleeping pills and a glass of water were on a small silver tray with claw feet. I was thinking as they rested on my tongue and suddenly the bitter taste of the drug came through and I hurriedly swallowed them down. When they hit the whisky my legs felt heavy and it took an effort to roll back on the bed as I sank into that merciful oblivion, the oblivion that starts a slow dissolve on a knife exploding in firm young flesh.

Gianni had sent a man to the airport to meet the first Alitalia flight from London and he was back at the via Torino about eleven with all the English newspapers.

There was nothing in any of them about Timonetti and I sat around the apartment all day reading Steinbeck's

Uomini e topi. I tuned in to the BBC for the midday news, but there was nothing. And there was nothing on the BBC's Overseas Service in Italian. The nine o'clock evening flight brought the two London evening papers. I missed it on the first run through but the second time I struck oil. It was a few lines in the stop-press column of the *Evening Standard*. Rather smudgy but just about legible.

LONDON GANG LINK WITH ITALY?
A report from Rome suggests a link between a London holdup gang involved in large-scale crime and Italian politicians in Milan. Further details are expected to be revealed in the next 24 hours.

I tuned in to the BBC ten o'clock news but Aunty was being her usual cautious self and probably doing a bit of checking before she put the stamp of her authority on such a vague item. But what mattered was that Guarini had got moving so quickly.

Gianni shook me awake at about four o'clock in the morning. He was grinning and pointing at the front page of *La Stampa*. There was a great big headline, '*Il partito nuovo accusato*', and a good solid piece. It mentioned no names but it listed about twenty big robberies in Britain and indicated a connection with important men in the new party. There was a guarded but acid comment from a Christian Democrat spokesman, a report of a refusal to comment on the 'tissue of lies' by the party Secretary of the Bandiera Nera and a statement from Scotland Yard that the matter was under investigation but was the responsibility of the Italian Police authorities. There was a hint of more revelations to come.

By the evening the *Corriere della Sera* had made it the main item and was hinting that the Milan police were covering up information and calling for an independent investigation. The two London evening papers had relegated it to foreign news and it got only a couple of inches. The BBC didn't mention it at all.

Gianni came into my room at about eight. He'd got the photographs and drawings of the villa. There were aerial views taken from a helicopter and shots from various angles that looked as if they'd been taken with a very long tele-lens. The plans of the building itself were very detailed and included the main items of furniture. The cable lines to the diesel generator were shown in red and the telephone lines were carefully marked in green. Gianni waited till I'd looked them over. He was sitting on the bed.

'It's worked, Max. Timonetti's place has been besieged by reporters and TV crews all day. He's losing his cool very fast. Blamed the police and his colleagues and he's cancelled the rally in Rome next week. Avvocato Franceschini was there for two hours and Timonetti's been making threats of a legal action against everybody from the newspapers to the President. At about four he went to the airport and was followed by a swarm of reporters and photographers. He took off heading in the direction of Switzerland in a private helicopter. They all think he's doing a flit to Zürich. The pilot registered a flight plan to Zürich and Vienna but they turned just before the frontier and circled back. He landed about five kilometres from the villa and went there in a Fiat van. He's holed up, Max, and we've got him.'

'When do we do it?'

'Tomorrow. Tomorrow night. We'll go down early tomorrow morning and we'll recce all day and go in when they've settled down for the night.'

'How many of your guys have you got in mind?'

'Two drivers, two cars, three others and you and me.'

'Can you get walkie-talkies?'

'Sure. No trouble at all. Just one other thing, Max.' He sounded embarrassed.

'What's that?'

'Will you see the old lady – Mama Mondadori – as she's making herself ill about the girl? She thinks she let you down and is desperate to see you.'

I'd known that this would have to happen some time. I wanted to know what had happened but I couldn't bear to hear the details. I'd rather have read a report, a medical report. I nodded at Gianni.

'OK, Gianni, you fix it.'

Mama Mondadori was in black and her big brown eyes had the haunted look of all those Jews, Poles and Russians who'd seen too much to ever look happy again. I kissed her and sat her on the bed. She had a rosary laced through the bony fingers of her left hand and she couldn't bring herself to look at me. I seemed to have spent a lifetime comforting people when I needed comforting myself. Why can't we take it in turns?

'Tell me what happened, Mama.'

She sighed and turned towards me.

'Signor Max, I grieve very much for the girl, but I

grieve for you too. I think you were happy with her. She cared about you very much. I have said many prayers for you both. I don't know why it all happened but I know they are evil men who can do things like that.' She rocked a little as she was speaking and her fingers touched the small crucifix.

'They came after we had eaten. I was in the kitchen washing up and when the bell rang I answered the door. There were two men, not big men, but one was very strong. They pushed inside and the other one held me with his hand over my mouth. The strong one moved very quietly like a cat. He looked in the other rooms and then went upstairs. I heard Tammy call out in fear and then she screamed, signor, and he must have put his hand over her mouth because I heard no more screams, just the noise of a struggle. Then after about ten minutes he came down. He didn't speak. Just nodded at the man holding me and then they left quickly. I heard a car door bang and an engine start. I think it was them.

'I think I knew she was killed, signor, and I was very frightened. I am an old woman now. I went up to your room and Tammy was across the bed. The sheets were wet with blood and there was blood on the walls. It was like a slaughterhouse. He had stabbed her many, many times and cut her in terrible ways. She was dead already. I covered her with some of my dresses and I telephoned for the police. They came very soon, signor, but it seemed a long, long time for me. I had no way to tell you. I didn't know where you were. I telephoned the British Consul but they thought I was just a mad woman. They were very polite but they didn't believe me.' She looked across at me, waiting for me to say my piece.

'Mama, there was nothing you could do. Nothing at all. It was a terrible thing and I shall not go back until they've paid for it. Can you tell me anything about the men? What they looked like? How they spoke?'

She threw up her hands.

'They never spoke one word, signor. Not one word all the time. But I will remember all my days what they looked like. The man who held me was older, about forty-five. Very dark skin and short hair like American soldiers. Very bad teeth and one of his ears was mis-shapen. Medium height and a bit fat. The other one was about thirty. Pale, sallow face and a Chinese moustache like journalists and pop stars have. Very black hair and he had eyes like an animal. Brown but pale brown, almost yellow. He moved always like a dancer. Quick but smooth and he always held his hands like fists. His fingers curled in and on his right hand his knuckles were swollen like a man with rheumatism. He seemed not only very strong but alert with his face and eyes like a bird.'

'And they didn't speak at all?'

'No, nothing. Except when he turned to go up the stairs he turned round and sort of spat but without spittle and it sounded like a word almost. But really just a sound.'

'Did he say it like this, Mama? *Sa!*'

Her hand moved to her mouth and there was fear in her eyes.

'Oh God, signor! Oh holy God! Yes, it was just like that. It frightens me even now when you do it. What is it? Some secret sign?'

'No, Mama. Forget it. It's just a foreign word. Don't think about it again.'

'And what are you going to do, signor. You are staying with Signor Podoni, so you are safe from the others?'

'Yes, I'm safe, Mama. Don't worry about me. I shall leave here when you leave and I shall go back to England in a few days. Is anybody worrying you, the police or the *carabinieri* or anyone?'

'No, Signor Podoni fixed all that. He tell them I am under his protection now.'

I gave her 100,000 lire, which sounds a fortune but is only sixty quid. I kissed both wet cheeks and took her down to Gianni. As I walked back to my room I could hear his voice as he started to tell her some story about a priest they both knew and one of his more expensive girls. Back in my room I poured a whisky and took it over to the table beside the bed. I lay down looking at the ceiling thinking of those terrible moments before Tammy had died. The fear, the hurt and the outrage. I was hot with anger and my face was beaded with perspiration and I wanted to shout out my rage. Then Gianni came in with a big oval tray of food. He had guessed how I would feel and he was going to get me back on the rails again. He put the tray on the low coffee table and came over and sat on the bed.

'You learn anything useful, Max?'

'Just one thing.'

'What's that?'

'I want to find one of Timonetti's razor boys who's spent time in Japan or maybe Okinawa. About thirty with a Fu Manchu moustache.'

'That's Gino. Gino Asti. He was five years in Japan.'

153

'What did he do there?'

'Ran a nightclub in Tokyo. It was owned by a consortium of Italians and Americans. He's been with Timonetti for a year now. He's got something wrong with his hand. Rheumatism or arthritis. Swollen joints.'

I shook my head. 'There's nothing wrong with his hand, Gianni. He's a karate buff. You get those big knuckles from using a Makiwara, a post with straw round it.'

'Mama Mondadori tell you this?'

'Sort of. She described how he walked and how he looked. And his hand. And she said he had said something like "*Sa*" before he went up to kill Tammy.'

'And what's that mean?'

'It's a word karate fighters use before they start. It means "let's go".'

'Sounds like a guy to avoid.'

'Can you check if he's gone with Timonetti to the villa?'

'Sure, I'll be back when I've made a call.'

While I waited I turned on the radio. They were playing a big orchestra version of 'Ebbtide' with waves and seagulls and several hundred harps and violins. I really was too old for these sort of games. Gianni's voice cut in on my thoughts.

'I'll know soon, Max. He's not at Timonetti's house anyway. Now, let's see.'

He clanged the silver lids off two dishes and the steam came up. There were gnolotti, pasta stuffed with meat – a sort of rich man's ravioli. There was a small bowl of those roasted chestnuts that Italians call castagne. The second dish was fileto all' Tartara, a

154

wonderful mixture of ground filet of beef, raw, mixed with raw egg, chopped onions and parsley. The sort of things they shovel into world class heavyweights the night before the big fight. We finished up with spumoni, a frozen dessert shaped like a heart with candied fruit.

Gianni was pouring out coffee when there was a knock at the door. He shouted, '*Si venga.*'

A girl put her head round the door and nodded at Gianni. He nodded back, '*Grazie.*' She closed the door and Gianni called out, 'Gioia, *un' momento.*' She came in and he waved at the remnants of our meal. 'Be a good girl and take this stuff away.'

She was about twenty, a pretty brunette, with a well-filled sweater and long, lovely legs. I opened the door for her as she manoeuvred the big tray through the narrow opening. When I sat down again Gianni said, 'You're smoking too much, *ragazzo.*'

'I always smoke too much, Gianni. Just one of those things.'

'You thought how you're going to leave this country?'

'By air?'

He shook his head and smiled. 'No, *ragazzo*. I've got influence but not total influence. Timonetti's group won't like what's happened. There'll be happy souls to take his place in the new party, that's for sure. But nobody can lay it on the line for all the police everywhere. There's a warrant out for your arrest for questioning. After tomorrow that will be withdrawn, but there'll still be people who would like you in the bag. I shall tell Guarini to lay off the day after tomorrow. That's my little present to the new boys. They'll sort themselves out in a day or two and things'll go back to normal.

But even the Christian Democrats would like to have you parcelled up in a jail in Roma, ready to talk about Timonetti's boys or else you get charged with the girl's murder. OK, you're found not guilty in the end but that's after two years in the nick. So you go quietly, Max. You agree?'

'Sure, whatever you say. But how?'

'Tomorrow one of my people is taking your boat at Santa Margherita for a little trip out into the bay, so that Mario can check the engines. When they get well out they will strike along the coast and by early afternoon they'll put her in Ventimiglia. You know Ventimiglia?'

'I've been there a couple of times.'

'OK, so she has some trouble and they lie up in the marina there. One of my drivers will take you down there when we have finished with Timonetti and you'll leave at once. Just go along to Nice or Menton and then you'll be safe, *ragazzo*.'

'Will there be any come-back against you when this is over, Gianni?'

'Nothing I can't handle.'

He was relaxed in his chair with his long legs stretched out and his feet crossed on the coffee table.

'I wonder what would have happened if we had become partners.'

He grinned. 'You'd have made a lot of dough, Max.'

'You like this life.'

He looked across at me with those warm eyes.

'I've got all the money I'll ever need. I've got the prettiest girls in every town north of Rome. I've got a large piece of the action in half a dozen legitimate businesses and all the action in most of the rackets this side of the Tiber.'

'And some day somebody's going to try to take it away.'

He grinned. 'They try it twice a year and they don't stand a chance. Let's talk about tomorrow.'

We checked over timings and distances and then stripped and reassembled the pistols and a flare gun. The walkie-talkies worked on a fixed frequency and provided no problem. When we had finished, Gianni went off. It was nearly midnight and we had an early start in the morning.

I was having a last whisky when the girl came in. She closed the door gently and walked over to the bed. It was the girl who had come in with the message for Gianni. She really was very beautiful.

'Hello, Signor Max. I've had orders from Gianni to stay with you tonight.'

'Your name's Gioia, isn't it?'

She laughed. 'No, it's Gaia; the Gioia bit is just Gianni's joke.'

'You'd better tell Gianni I'm not in the mood. Not even for beauties like you.'

She didn't look offended. Just walked over and helped herself to a whisky.

'I can't tell Gianni, he's gone to the cathedral. He warned me anyway.'

'Why's he gone to the cathedral?'

'To pray of course. He is much concerned about you. There is much pressure everywhere to find you. They would certainly kill you if they got the chance.'

Gianni praying in the cathedral was a new Gianni to

me. Maybe the air of confidence and security was for my benefit. Maybe the pressures were more than I guessed. I looked up at the girl.

'I really do think you're beautiful but I don't want to sleep with anyone tonight.'

She nodded her head. 'Don't worry. Gianni told me about the girl. I understand. He understands you too. He said you would be lonely tonight and I must stay with you. If you like to make love with me, I like it too. If not, I still sleep in your bed.'

She put down her glass and walked over to the bath-room. I heard the bathwater running and almost half an hour later she came out, naked and glowing. She smiled and stood still and I couldn't help looking at the full breasts and the black fleece between her legs. Then she walked over to me.

'Come on, Signor Max. Let's get you undressed and in bed. You need your sleep tonight.'

We lay in the bed together and her hand held mine. She told me the folk story of the man who shot a nightingale and then sang very softly a gentle little love song – '*Roma non far la stupida stasera*'. I put my arm under her slender neck and she turned towards me with her soft yielding warmth. Two minutes later she was asleep and I could relax with my nightmares of knives and blood and Tammy.

Eleven

Four in the morning is a time for doing, not thinking. If you're not sleeping, that is. I dressed and shaved and gathered up my few things. The girl was still sleeping and her dark lashes were ridiculously long as they swept the contours of her cheeks. One hand was under the pillow, the other was under her cheek and her fine black hair trailed over the pillow like some delicate lichen. Her neat rump made an exciting shape under the sheet. With all the contrariness of the human condition I could have made love to her there and then. No trouble at all. Wash your scruples in sleep and all will be well. I didn't feel old any more.

When I went down the passage Gianni's door was open. There were five men around the table and Gianni pointed to a vacant chair for me. The butler was serving breakfast – English style: rashers of lean bacon, fried eggs and fried bread. There were big cups of steaming coffee and the men looked me over as they ate.

'Max, I'll go round the table starting on your left. Giuseppe knows more about cars than any man I know except Tomasso who's sitting next to him. Then on my

159

left here, Francesco, then the pretty one with curls is Vincenzo and, finally, the ugly man who gets all the girls, Luciano.'

They all nodded in turn and got on with their food. Gianni was at the coffee stage and he looked relaxed. He leaned back and pushed his plate to one side.

'I want to leave in fifteen minutes. Max, you'll be with me and Giuseppe. The others will go in the van. There's food and water in the van and automatic rifles and ammunition. I want to leave the autostrada half-way to Piacenza and we drop Vincenzo there with a walkie-talkie. He'll report on the hour what he sees from the front of the villa. The rest of us take the side roads and work along to the other side of the hill. We can get both vehicles almost to the top and then there's a copse of oaks and chestnuts, and we can camouflage the car and the van. When we've finished Giuseppe will take you and the car to the boat. It'll be a long journey to avoid the coast road. Maybe five or six hours. You, Giuseppe, will do whatever Signor Max tells you to do. His orders are my orders, understood?'

Giuseppe looked at me and nodded.

'Right, now. We've no set plan so a few precautions. When Signor Max goes in the villa you shoot anybody who approaches from the main road. Anybody from the orchards you bring to me at the generator house. If Timonetti tries to leave, you kill him. If Gino Asti tries to leave, you kill him too. Nobody leaves that villa. Understand?'

He looked at each one in turn and they nodded their agreement.

'Next thing. If anything goes very wrong and we all

get split up you don't come back here, you make your way to Genova. You go to the restaurant and stay there till you get orders what to do. If we get involved with the police you ask for Avvocato Lunghi and you don't talk till he comes. If we get stuck with the *carabinieri* you ask for Capitano Vitali at Milan. You don't talk except to him. In your jackets you've each got an envelope. Each envelope contains 100,000 lire and twenty US dollars. Use it if you need it. Max, there's an anorak jacket for you. It will be cold for some hours yet. You'll need it.'

Gianni pointed at Tomasso.

'Tomasso, you and your people go now. You'll be slower. Leave the door open downstairs for us. OK, off you go.'

There was a canvas satchel for me and I put it over my shoulder as we stood at the door downstairs. A dark blue Alfa was standing there and we went down the steps and into the car one by one. I was last man out. Gianni went before me and he crossed himself as he went through the door. We headed north round the Parco Sempione and I thought of when Tammy and I had sat by the lake and watched the children playing. Then we went past the Garibaldi Station and into the one-way system that took us to the ring road. We turned right at the ring road and went 180 degrees around Milan until we hit the road to Piacenza. The sun was rising behind us but there was mist both sides of the road. There was little traffic on the roads, a few lorries leaving Milan with meat and vegetables and a bus or two taking in workers for the six o'clock shifts in the big Milan industrial complexes. There were quail feeding on the grass verges and I saw a vixen waiting to cross the wide road, alert and ragged-coated from her cubs. Where we turned off the autostrada the road narrowed and curved to pass under the main road. Almost at once the winding road clung to the side of a hill and the mist was below us in the valley. I could see the tops of cypresses and poplars standing ghost-like above the white vapour. Beside the road the earth was golden and red; on the sandstone outcrops clusters of small alpine elder were covered with their bunches of scarlet berries. There were the big yellow heads of yellow adonis and the bright blood red berries of pheasant's eye opening wide in the sun.

A few big gates and high walls indicated the solitary houses that marked a small village here and there. And now the slopes were calmer and there were the first cultivated areas of olives and a vineyard or two. Gradually the heat of the sun penetrated the car and condensation ran down the windows. Nearly an hour after leaving the autostrada the car nosed up a rough stony path and into the shade of a plantation of chestnuts, oaks and birches. Then Giuseppe turned in a tight circle and the car again faced the road. It was 7.10 and a lot would happen before the car went down the path again.

Giuseppe stayed with the car and Gianni and I walked through to the other side of the copse. There was flowering broom on the slope of the hill and then the dead ground hid everything. Near the last of the bushes Gianni stopped and waved me down. We crawled to the edge of the gentle slope and where the ground fell steeply were the olives and peaches and the red roof of the villa. It lay in a bowl of the mountain and looked bigger than I remembered, and more peaceful.

Gianni passed me the binoculars and I rested my elbows on the anorak. There was a Lancia Flavia parked near the garage but there was nobody moving that I could see, although there was a wisp of smoke from one of the chimneys. Probably the kitchen. The generator house was hidden by the far edge of the roof and the foam of bougainvillaea. We made our way round the rim of the bowl and from the lower viewpoint we could see the patio through the glasses. It was still in shade; the sun had not yet come from behind the hill. A man sat on a camp stool with a shotgun across his knees. He looked across the panorama of the valley. It must have been impossible for him to see anyone approaching until they were within ten yards of him. It was an hour before anyone else came out on to the patio. Then it was Gino Asti and, as I put the glasses on him, I saw that Mama Mondadori's description was very accurate. He was wearing a bright yellow dressing gown with an ornate red dragon emblazoned on its back. His sallow flat face looked Chinese, enhanced by the thin black eyebrows that covered his piggy eyes. He was standing barefoot with his hands in the dressing gown pockets. He was moving slightly, pivoting on his waist rather like an impatient boxer waiting to go into the ring. He was talking and laughing with the guard, and he took his right hand out of his pocket to emphasize a point and his fingers were outstretched in karate style as he lunged forward at his imaginary opponent. But I noticed one good thing. His left heel came up off the ground as he turned. You don't get to even first

Dan with technique like that. Whatever the Karateka say, karate is for killing, but it only works if the co-ordination and control are perfect. Less than perfect and you're very vulnerable. And your true Karateka would never laugh while he demonstrated or worked. Even showing your teeth is a beginner's crime. I reckoned I could show Asti a thing or two.

Then as I watched I saw the girl. She was wearing a pale blue bikini. A thin strip across the full breasts and a small triangle at her hips. Asti turned round and eyed her and said something to her. She shrugged, laughing and, encouraged, Asti strutted around shadow boxing, what the Italians dismissively describe as 'cutting a figure'. Then Timonetti came out, dressed in a white shirt and blue cotton slacks. He stood hands on hips looking at Asti's posturing in front of the girl. He said something, and Asti subsided and did a pseudo-salute and went inside.

All morning we watched the villa but there was very little movement until just before midday when an open truck pulled up and three men jumped out. The truck turned and went back down the rocky road. The men went round to the back of the villa. Timonetti came out and stood speaking with them and then pointed to the area of the olive trees and peaches. The men were carrying old-fashioned sub-machine guns. They looked like old Berettas, either 38/42s or 38As; it was impossible to identify them positively, but I thought I could see the vent holes in the fat round barrels. They handled them clumsily like gangsters in old films. One man stayed at the rear of the villa and the other two moved off into the olive trees in opposite directions. We watched carefully for an hour but neither man came out beyond the olive groves.

Giuseppe relieved us at two o'clock and we walked back to the car. Giuseppe had camouflaged it skilfully but not obviously; branches of trees had been bent but not broken and free use had been made of the soft shadows of the taller trees. We sat, eating cheese sand-wiches and tomatoes.

'We could go in as soon as it's dark, Gianni. Why wait around until they're in bed?'

Gianni stopped in mid-bite and shook his head.

'No, *ragazzo*. There're two parts to this operation, just like the old days. The first part is to deal with Asti and Timonetti, and the second is for us all to get away safely. If a man gets away in the early evening, he can cause trouble. If he gets away around midnight, he would take hours to get anything moving.'

'Are you going back to Milan, Gianni?'

'No, I'm going back up to Brescia. I've got a refrig-erator plant up there. Time to look them over.'

We slept for three hours and then took over from Giuseppe. He told us there had been little movement at the villa but a light van bearing the name of a grocer in Piacenza had delivered two large cardboard boxes and an open wooden case holding tins that looked like food. He also handed over letters, newspapers and a large cylinder of butane gas.

By seven the sun was behind us and we lay low on the edge of the hollow. An hour later the guards went down. It looked as if they had gone in to eat. It was almost ten when the guards came out again, this time at the front of the villa.

Gianni had arranged for his men to assemble at the car as soon as the light started going, and I made my way round the bowl of the hill to the far side of the villa. There was better cover that side and the slope curved round to encompass the garage and generator house. Timonetti's guards were sitting on a wooden bench smoking and talking. As I wound my way carefully down the slope I could hear faint music from a radio. There were four or five gorse bushes in full bloom and I settled down to watch from the foremost clump. I could see the transistor radio through the glasses and the three men were pulling on rough sheepskin jackets. Half an hour later the light had gone and the moon was still low. A ground mist was curling up in the olive grove but the warmth of the building kept a clear area by the villa. But the white fronds would roll down the slope to the building as the temperature fell rapidly in the next hour.

Two of the guards moved off into the trees and the third patrolled slowly along the back of the villa. Gianni and his three henchmen moved in alongside me shortly afterwards. The drivers were back at the vehicles and Giuseppe had one of the walkie-talkies. We settled down for the long wait.

Just before midnight Gianni and I moved down to the back of the garage where the telephone line came down to ground level. There was a thick rubber sheathing and I pared that away in a thick band down to the cable itself. If I cut the cable and they tried to use the phone they would know it had been cut and then they'd be alerted. But there was a thing you could do with telephone cables that still kept the dialling tone but closed off the rest of the circuit. It would take ten minutes to fix, and if they tried the phone in that time they might rumble what was going on. And if you touched the bare wire before you'd made the connection it could raise a tinkle back at the phone. I made a deep cut in each cable insulation and then worked the soft plastic back with my fingers. I could smell the shellac in the clear fresh air. If it was solid copper, I couldn't do it, and I ran my nail slowly along the cable to test the surface. As I brought it back it grated on the mesh of wires and I knew I could do it. I used one of the china insulators where the cable was held to the garage wall and laced the cat's cradle of wires till they held against the pull of the cable. The wires were hot and I swathed them in the rubber sheathing. It would work for two hours and then it would burn itself out.

There was only one light on now in the villa, in the service room that the guards were using. We crept back to the gorse bushes. We waited until one o'clock and then Gianni nodded at one of his men and passed him a silencer. We took off our jackets and the man slid his pistol and the silencer underneath them and there was only the faintest click as he pushed it home. Then he moved off, crouching low as he left the shelter of the gorse bushes. We had reckoned it would take him an hour to deal with the guard on the far side, but he was back in forty minutes. He nodded to Gianni as he handed over the pistol. The guard nearest to us must have been very near because we heard the faint 'pfut' of the compressed air and then it came again. Gianni was breathing heavily when he got back. But it was going to plan.

We stayed flat on the ground, Luciano, Gianni and I, as we edged our way down and across the back of the villa. The moon was up now and the mist had rolled right down the hill to the bougainvillaea. The guard was leaning against the wall beside the door. Gianni pressed a pebble into my hand and grinned as he went off to the right. Luciano was already in the shadow of the generator house. I strained my eyes to keep sight of the pale disc of Gianni's face, lost it, and then saw the white of a spread handkerchief. It fluttered twice and I pitched the pebble to the left of the guard. He hesitated for a moment and then unshipped his gun and walked towards the noise. Gianni had his arm across his face and wrenched the machine gun upwards and outwards and we heard it thud and rattle on the grass. The guard was well-built and it took two of us to move his body into the first row of olives.

This was the part we had planned very carefully, since this was the part that could easily have gone wrong. There were three of us and three of them. The girl, Timonetti and my man. But we were not sure where they were. The girl we could guess about but the other two were unpredictable. We had planned for me to go in first. Gianni would come in from the front and Luciano would cover me from behind, and he would also control the girl.

I went in the service room as Gianni went round to the front. Beyond was the kitchen and I moved through carefully. I grasped the big wooden knob on the door firmly and turned it slowly. I pushed it open and moved quietly into the main living room, and as I did the lights came on. Timonetti was standing there. He was holding a pistol which was pointed at me and nodding his patrician head as if he were agreeing with something I had said.

'Put down the gun, Signor Farne. No, down. Just let it fall. We can stand the noise.' I let it fall and it bounced and slid under an armchair by the fireplace. He waved his pistol in the direction of the other chair.

'Sit down, signor. I assume you have others with you. We'll wait for them, shall we?'

He walked slowly over to the telephone and lifted the receiver. He tucked it under his jaw and dialled. Then he jerked at the cradle. He was getting a dialling tone but it wouldn't dial. He tried it again and then slowly put the receiver back on its cradle. There had been no sound from Gianni or Luciano. Luciano must have heard everything that had happened.

Timonetti walked slowly across the room and rapped on the door of the room where I had slept.

'Asti, *avanti, vieni qui.*'

Asti came out struggling into the yellow dressing gown. He didn't notice me at first and then Timonetti nodded in my direction.

'That is the Englishman Farne.'

The hood looked at me, hands on hips, taking in my size but relying on my grey hair. He stared with his big dark eyes and then half-smiled as he worked out all the sums. Timonetti interrupted the beautiful thoughts.

'Lock the girl's room, Asti.'

The man almost glided across to the girl's door, opened it slightly, reached in for the key, removed it and then turned it in the lock.

0

'Check the kitchen, Asti, and the guards' room. Then call them back down here.'

Luciano would get him if he was lucky. But Asti moved through the rooms. I heard him switching out lights, and then he was outside, bellowing for the guards to report back.

Timonetti stood waiting until Asti came back. Asti's sallow face had a worried look. He looked at me first as if that might solve the mystery and then reluctantly turned to Timonetti.

'*Non c'e nessuno*, Signor Dino.'

Gianni must have pulled back his troops to keep Timonetti guessing. The snag as far as I was concerned was that Timonetti might guess wrong and knock me off. Timonetti walked towards me and when he was about six feet away there was a crash of glass, the 'pfft' of a silencer and a piece of the tiled floor came up in fragments. The bullet ricocheted to the far wall and went off on another tangent to clatter into one of the cast-iron garden chairs by the fireplace. Timonetti had slow reflexes and he turned with his gun the wrong way, facing the back of the villa. I went for his legs and his head clipped the glass-topped table as he fell. The gun dropped and I scrambled to reach for it. I almost had my hand over it when Asti's bare foot took me in the throat. For a moment I couldn't breathe and then there was a pounding brilliant red behind my eyes. I heard glass breaking and voices. The room tilted and then righted itself, and I was on my knees still holding the gun. As I stood up I saw a man with a gun; it was Gianni and the gun was covering Asti who had his back to the wall.

Luciano came in from the kitchen and grinned at me. Gianni called out to him to take over Asti. When Gianni had handed over, he came across to me.

'You all right, *amico*?'

'Not bad, Gianni. What happened?'

'I pulled the boys round to the front and then I saw Timonetti going for you so I fired through the window and came in. That little whore Sylva got out through the bedroom window. One of the boys is searching for her now. Let's have a look at Timonetti.'

Timonetti had blood pouring down one side of his face from a wound on his forehead. His other eye was open and he was breathing all right as we rolled him on to his back. I slid my hands under his shoulders and lifted him into one of the big armchairs. He weighed very little and his head and shoulders slumped forward almost to his knees. I put my hand under his chin and pushed him back. Gianni came back with a bowl of water and a towel. He slung the water at Timonetti's face and he came up gasping and choking, flailing his arms. He looked at us both, trying to remember what had happened. Then the light dawned and he struggled to stand up. I pushed him back and he looked at Gianni. His voice quavered as he spoke but it still held faint echoes of authority.

'What are you doing here, Podoni?'

Gianni smiled a grim smile. 'I'm the friend of a friend, Dino.'

'A friend of a friend. What friend? What does it mean?'

'A friend of a friend of Tammy Walton, Dino.'

Timonetti looked up at him as if I wasn't there, one big man to another.

171

'But surely something can be arranged, Signor Podoni. This is not necessary,' and he swept his thin arm to encompass the broken glass and the blood on his face. Gianni wasn't smiling any more.

'See what you can do, Timonetti. He's the boss,' and he jerked his hand in my direction. The thin, hawk-like face turned to me and the shrewd eyes looked into mine. He opened his mouth to speak but I shook my head.

'What happened to Dixon, Timonetti?'

He folded his hands carefully as if he were at a board meeting, ready to explain how last year was a year of reorganization but no profits. He nodded his head as if he'd made the big decision.

'That's what you want to know, Mr Farne.'

'That's what I want to know.'

The old eagle face had a lean little smile of super-iority. The sort of smile experienced politicians have when the interviewers ask their opponent a nasty question. His thin fingers came together as if in prayer.

'You didn't know much about Dixon, did you?'

'No.'

'He was a strange mixture, Signor Farne. Considerable ability. A successful operator in the textile business and in his other business enterprises too. But when you have an arrangement you'd best stick to it. Especially in some areas of business. Now Signor Dixon started playing games on his own. He kept money that didn't belong to him. You know what I mean, I'm sure. And when the pressure was applied he thought he could see me and make some arrangement. It was not possible, Signor Farne. It would never have been possible, but

172

at that particular moment it could have been disastrous to plans of mine. Plans that had been made and carried out over years. Things that were more important than any one man. Dixon came to see me and I told him so. We quarrelled and I told him that he had twenty-four hours to get the money across here. He neither agreed to do it nor disagreed, but I am sure he knew what the consequences would be if he went on playing silly games. I think he fully understood my determination about this. But equally I think he underrated my influence.'

'So you had him killed?'

His sharp eyes looked at me and the little superior smile came back. He shook his head.

'No, Signor Farne. As it happens, I didn't have him killed. I had him under surveillance and I would have had him killed. However, my man lost contact with him. I assumed he had gone to Santa Margherita to the boat he had talked about. I sent down Signor Dodds to deliver a note. You know what happened. And I think you took the note. It was not in his personal effects handed to the police.'

He looked at me as if he expected an answer.

'So what happened to Dixon?'

'Signor Dixon had gone to a club. A private club called the one-six-five. As you probably know, Signor Farne, that is the number of the German State law that covers homosexuality. Signor Dixon was a very attractive man to both sexes and it seems he made a conquest that night. An unfortunate conquest as it turned out. The boy concerned was the lover of a very unstable man. Signor Dixon was followed to a house used by homosexuals and that is where he was killed. His fate was waiting for him there.'

It was all too obviously true and it tied up all the loose ends that had been hanging around. Tammy would be surprised when I told her about the homosexual bit, but it fitted even her experience with Dixon. And then I remembered she was dead. I turned to Gianni.

'Do you believe him?'

He thought for a moment and then nodded and said quietly, 'Yes, I believe him.'

And I shot Timonetti as he opened his mouth to speak. The impact of the bullet jerked his head but the wound was just a small circle over his left eye. A small hole and a small trickle of dark red blood. He died instantly.

I turned and went over to Luciano and pushed him aside. I gripped Asti's bathrobe and pulled him close. Gianni was right beside me.

'Let me fix him, Max. You've had enough, *amico*, and it's getting late.'

I shook my head and smashed my fist into Asti's face. His hands came up and closed over my right arm. His yellow eyes were like the eyes of a wolf. I jack-knifed and came up with my head under his jaw. I heard the crunch as his teeth smashed together but he still held my right arm. I turned and bent to take him over my shoulder and he loosed my arm and both his hands clawed my face. I went back against him to take off the pressure. I stamped to find his instep but he moved his feet and hooked my leg. I took him with me as I went down and I heard his head crash as it hit the tiled floor. I felt hands pulling me off him, but I wrenched myself free and got my hands in his hair and beat his head against the tiles till I passed out.

When I came to I was on the back seat of a car and it was daylight. All my body ached and my hands felt as if they had been burned. As I struggled to sit up, the car door opened. It was Luciano. His face was grey with exhaustion.

'How do you feel now, signor?'

'I'm OK. Where are Gianni and the others?'

'It took a long while to bring you round, signor. You were very bad. It was getting light and it was important that Gianni should leave. He gave me instructions what to do. And a letter for you, signor.'

He pulled down the cover of the glove compartment and held out an envelope. I reached out for it and it was as though somebody had stuck a red-hot poker up my arm. And then I noticed my hands were bound up in wet cloth. Luciano said quietly, 'Let me open it for you, Signor Max.' He ripped open the envelope and flattened the stiff blue paper. I leaned against the side of the car and read it slowly.

Dear Max,

I have to go off now. It took longer than I planned for. There are some problems. I have given L orders and he will tell you what they are and carry them out. He will arrange for you to see a doctor. The fingers of your hand that was damaged at S.M. are very bad. Your other hand is only swollen so far as I can see. When you get back to England you must have a proper check-up. Asti died when he first went down so all accounts are squared.

175

But I was very sad for you. I still am. I shall pray for you and shall arrange for a mass to be said for the girl. It is all a waste.

This does not square our personal account, I am still in your debt. When things settle down after this I shall come over and see you, *amico.* We will paint London or whatever it is you say.

    Ciao e augure
    Gianni.

I leaned my head back against the window and I saw Luciano's unshaven face spin and dissolve as the pain flowed over me again. It was dark again when I came round and I could smell cigarette smoke. As I stirred, I heard Luciano.

'Don't move, Signor Max. There's not long to wait now.'

'What are we waiting for?'

Luciano turned and put a cigarette to my lips. They were numb and puffed out as though I had had a session at the dentist. He held the cigarette while I drew on it.

'Christ, it's cold, Luciano! Where are we?'

'Just outside La Spezia, signor.'

'God! We're supposed to be at the boat. Mario will be waiting for us.'

'Don't worry, signor. Gianni will have spoken to Mario on the telephone. He is coming here to take care of you.'

'How will he know where to find us?'

'This was one of Gianni's places in the war. There is a restaurant not far away. He will be here very soon.'

'Are we on the main road, Luciano?'

'No, signor, we are up a mountain road below the Passo del Cerreto.'

I remembered the name from partisan reports but I'd never been there. The Germans had tried to patrol the area but they'd given up early on.

As I woke I heard voices. They were very low but I recognized Mario's and I called his name. My voice sounded like one of the bullfrogs on the Pontine marshes. The door swung open and Mario knelt on the front seat. He wasted no time.

'Max, we've got a long ride. We're going to my place for a few days until you're better. Can you take it?'

'Sure I can take it, but it's not necessary. Just take me to the boat.'

'Max, I'm doing what Gianni ordered. You can't take a boat out as you are, and you've got to lie low until the panic dies down.'

'Has there been anything in the papers about Timonetti?'

'No idea. I've got too much to do to read papers.'

'How long will it take us?'

'Just over an hour.'

There was little traffic as we followed the coast road and Santa Margherita was empty as we went down to the Piazza and turned right up the hill to Mario's villa. Mafalda was waiting for us and when I was in bed she brought me a bowl of soup and sat on the bed watching me eat.

'I'm sorry about all this nuisance, Mafalda. I'll be fit tomorrow and I'll get on my way.'

She smiled her calm smile and patted my face.

'You'll go when Mario says, my dear, and not until.'

For three days I slept and sat in the sun in the garden. No radio, no papers, no nothing. They wouldn't talk about Timonetti. I could understand. The fewer people involved the better. The doctor came each day and cut the dressings off my hands and checked the joints and re-covered them in plaster of Paris. At the end of a week even the sticking plaster came off. The joints were still swollen but I could use my hands clumsily.

We were having dinner on the Sunday evening when Mario raised the subject of my departure.

'I'll take you tomorrow, Max. We'll cross the border at Pont Saint Louis. Use your Irish passport. There'll be no trouble; you'll be just another tourist.'

'Maybe I'll phone Gianni before I go.'

Mario had his fork halfway to his mouth. He slowly put it down and looked at his plate for a moment. Then he looked up at me and shook his head. 'I shouldn't do that, Max. The police are pretty active at the moment. Anyway, I've no idea where he is.'

'Is the boat still at Ventimiglia?'

'No, we got it moved to the marina at Cap Martin. It means you're already over the frontier there. She's fuelled and provisioned but you'll need to take on water. No good letting it get stale in the tanks. By the way, it's the last place you get free water before Toulon. You'll have to pay at Nice and Cannes.'

* * *

178

As Mario had said, we went over the frontier at midday without any passport problems. The Fjord was clean and shiny and it was like coming home. Mario sat with me at the saloon table and we drank a half bottle of Chianti. He went over the stores with me. I checked that I still had my money. Mario had bought me duty-free diesel coupons so I was all set. It was almost four when I waved Mario off.

I stripped off the hood that covered the aft cockpit area and it was a tonic to be checking over a boat again. I started with the batteries and fixed the charger. I checked the fuel in both tanks and they were full. I uncovered the water hose and it took an hour to fill both tanks. I left the charger coupled but switched off when I tested the engines. They both fired and took first time. I let them idle for ten minutes and then killed them. I checked the main marine bands on the radio. All was well.

I was sitting in the cockpit when a boy came along the quayside. He had a bottle in his hand and he was looking at the names painted on the sterns of the boats. He bent down and read the name on the Fjord's fat transom. Then he looked at me.

'Monsieur Farne?'

'Oui, j'y suis.'

He smiled and waved the bottle dangerously.

'C'est pour vous, la bouteille.' And he bent down holding out the bottle. It was 1966 Moët et Chandon. And taped to the bottle was an envelope.

I reached up with a couple of francs for the boy.

The envelope came off easily and I read what was written on it.

A Monsieur Max Farne
MV *Lucky Penny*
Rue du Quai.

Drink the champagne tonight before you leave.
Read the note inside *only* when you are in sight
of the harbour at Chichester. Mario and Mafalda

I gave the harbour-master my cruising plan and ETA
at Nice and went back to the boat. With the engine
idling I held the boat to the pontoon with a boat-hook
and cast off both lines. There was an ebbing tide and
she was making twelve knots as she came to the
promontory of the cape itself. I was standing off about
half a mile but I could see car lights on the coast road.
The road wound back on itself as it went up the spine
of the cape through the wealthy estates with their olives
and myrtles. There were lights flickering up on the hill
at Cabbe or Roquebrune. I set the Sharps Pilot for the
course to Cap Ferrat. I poured out some of the champagne and I began to feel good.

It took seventeen days to get to the Channel but I'd
had a few days of rest thrown in. The weather was beginning to break as it always does when we get to the hump
of the summer. As I tied up at Barfleur, Niton Radio
was giving out a gale warning for Portland and Wight.
I stayed there two days and then headed for Chichester.
We locked through into Birdham Pool and I chugged
round and tied up alongside *Sally*. It was two days later
when I was transferring my kit from *Lucky Penny* that
I noticed Mario's envelope. I stopped and slit it open
with a screwdriver, and sat down with a beer to read it.

Dear Max,

I hope you had a safe, easy voyage back home. It can be very lonely on such a long sea voyage on your own, and I did not want you to have this news to think about on your journey.

Gianni Podoni was killed after leaving the villa. The Pellozzi girl got away and contacted people in Milan. They put a group on the autostrada to Milan and one on the autostrada to Brescia. There was little traffic on the road that early and they sandwiched his car and he was gunned down. He died in hospital in Brescia an hour after he was admitted.

This was why we kept you from the newspapers and the radio. He was not my kind of man, but I know you liked him, and you were a hero for him.

There has been much unhappiness this time for you but you must accept it and get back to normal.

The chaos about Timonetti has died down and is put at Gianni's door. Nevertheless I think you should wait six months or so before you come back here, even on business.

Gianni was buried in Naples and there were many people at the service.

Let me know what you want me to do about the various transactions here. I can drive a hard bargain buying boats for you, but I can't sell like you can.

Mafalda and I send you our love,
Ciao, Mario.

*   *   *

I sold the Fjord to an architect from Midhurst a couple of days later. I spent another two therapeutic days straightening things out on *Sally*. I got the MGC out of the garage at Chichester and on the Thursday *Sally* went across to the boatyard to be slipped and scraped. Then I headed for London.

I booked myself in at Brown's in Dover Street. I needed the dark sedateness. After lunch I settled down at the telephone. A rather snooty girl PRO at the Stock Exchange informed me that they never gave details of individual members but James Bravington was in *Who's Who*. I strolled across to Hatchards and looked up Bravington. His house was at Limpsfield in Surrey.

The village of Limpsfield lies at the foot of the Downs. The village itself is a cluster of shops and houses that merge with middle-class Oxted. There was an old man scything the grass in the churchyard where it sloped towards a field of barley. At the beginning of the end of summer the long grass was dry and brown but there were bright red spots of corn poppies and the pale blue of cornflowers. I walked over to the old man and, as I got near him, he straightened up and pushed his cap back on his head and kept his hand on the peak as he looked at me. Then he pointed past me, where I'd come from.

'It's back yonder,' he said, 'but you'll have to ask Vicar if you want to take pictures of it.'

I shook my head. 'No, I don't want to take pictures.'

He squinted across at me in the bright sunlight, and his quick observant country eyes held some doubt.

'You're looking for the Delius grave, aren't you?'

'No, I didn't know he was buried here.'

'Oh, yes. Him an' his wife. They all comes to look, you know, but they don't put no flowers on the grave.' He chuckled. 'One of those fellows from London he told me he died of the clap, but I reckon he must be pullin' my leg. Now what was you lookin' for, mister?'

'I was looking for a new grave. A girl. Tammy Walton.'

He frowned and scratched his head. 'Don't recognize the name but there's been half a dozen this last month.'

'Her stepfather is James Bravington. Lives at Mead House in Detillens Lane.'

'Oh yes, you're right, now I come to think of it. Yes. A young gal she was, they brought her back from Africa or somewhere. Been killed by foreigners. It's over there by the rowan trees. See, the ones with the red berries. They was late this year. You'll see it when you get there.'

'Thanks.'

He returned to his scything and I walked round the edge of the churchyard to the rowan trees. And there it was. Just a gentle, rounded oblong mound of earth and a tatty indestructible wreath, splotched from rain and mud, and a card that had been typed at the florists. 'To Tammy dear from Mummy and Daddy.' They'd played it as low-profile as they could. No love, no grief, just genteel convention. I toyed with going along to the house. 'Mummy' might have a photograph of Tammy and I'd have liked that. But I didn't go.

I did one more check while I was in London. I phoned the Pembury hospital. Mavis Trevor had been discharged and was being nursed at her home.

*   *   *

When I got back to Birdham Pool there were half a dozen letters and a small package from Italy. I opened the package first. There was a note from Mario.

Dear Max,
The jeweller's shop delivered this today. Tammy bought it for you but left it for them to engrave.
Love,
Mario

'This' was a silver cigarette lighter. On the side, carefully inscribed were the words from the song I'd asked for that evening in Rapallo.

'Un sol' amore, e questo sei tu'. T.W.

I hoped that she knew what it meant.